Seasons

[a collection of poems and stories]

By Ashton Pacholski

Second Printing, 2021

ISBN: 978-0-578-62779-3

To Mom and Pop—*siempre*.

Forward

(clears throat)

Hmm.

To be honest, dear reader, it's quite strange typing this introduction. I don't know why, but I've been hesitant to do so. I mean, how does one begin a forward to their first book? What do I even say?

Howdy?

No, that's not it.

That's too informal.

Hmm.

(drinks water)

Maybe I should I go over the book?

Eventually.

Maybe I should write about my childhood?

Irrelevant.

Hmm.

Sorry, dear reader. By now you're probably wondering: *why am I reading this guy's neurotic ramblings? Did he really just take a drink in the middle of his forward? Is he going to go somewhere with all this? Did I leave my stove on this morning?*

Well, I hope not, dear reader. For your sake and mine.

And rest assured—*here we go*—I think I've finally found the right words to say.

Ready?

(clears throat)

Hello.

Now—*moving along*—someone once said to me that poetry is not a competition; however, it's an invitation. And I like to think this collection best represents that idea.

With that being said, dusting off this proverbial bar stool next to me: *welcome…this round is on me.*

As you read through this collection, I hope you find enjoyment. Even if it's just momentary escapism as you relax on a work break, or get ready for a coffee shop date, then that's perfect.

(smiles)

Because, dear reader, **Seasons** operated much the same for me over the span of a year—giving me an escape when I needed it the most—and for that I am grateful.

The poems and stories that follow don't really have a predictable course. Much like a maple tree with shifting leaves, from a verdant green to a bright yellow, these works are deciduous (changing). As you evolve through these pages, new layers will be removed, and others—much like leaves in a crisp, fall breeze—will be revealed.

And listen—*I know.*

For some, poetry isn't the most digestible genre of literature. And if you relate to that, then no problem. Please regard the stories in the back. However, regarding poetry's general appeal, I understand some of the pushback. Sometimes an ambiguity creeps in. Sometimes we just want the roses red, the violets blue, and the sugar…well, you know.

But, like I said before, poetry is an invitation. The aim is often universal; although, more often than not, a literary work becomes a personal reflection.

A subconscious projection so to speak.

And any resonance thereafter with the public is a counted blessing. However—*and this is probably the English teacher in me speaking*—I've included some poetic devices and tools on the next page for your reading (*and possible analysis*).

Although, as you begin **Seasons**, do what you will with these works, and regardless of your reading toolbox, my only request for you, dear reader, is to *enjoy*. To sit back, relax—maybe get some coffee—and take a look into the seasons of a life: my first collection.

I'm glad you're here.

And lastly, before I let you go, maybe you'll find some commonalities and realizations with me here. Maybe we'll even find each other one day and discuss them.

If so...
...I'll smile once again...
...with a familiar voice...
...and say...
(clears throat)

Hello.

With love,
Ashton

TOOLS FOR YOUR READING TOOLBOX*

Metaphor: a comparison made between two things that would seemingly be unrelated to fully express the meaning of some idea, usually stylistically. "The *sky* was an *ocean*." Both nouns in the example are respectively different but share comparative qualities, i.e., blueness and scope.

Simile: *similar to the metaphor*, this is a comparison made between two things to derive a clearer idea using the terms "like" or "as." "The sky was *like* an ocean."

Personification: the figurative act of giving inanimate objects (such as a chair, a pistol, a moon, etc.) human qualities or abilities. *I often asked my students what would happen if their pencils started talking to them randomly. Their responses never failed to bring a smile to my face.*

Repetition: the repeating of words or phrases often used to add emphasis or rhythm. *I like to think this tool adds a nice musicality to a poem. Here's to you, Shel.*

Enjambment: this tool suggests reading two lines of poetry—regardless of ending punctuation—as one connected thought/phrase. Often times, reading with enjambment can change a perspective entirely. *Regard the poem "Eventually" in this collection.*

---

*If this poetical jargon hasn't bored you, and you crave additional tools, I'd say use your phone, a poetic manual (*if those exist*), or some digital device to help you find some more. However, these five will suffice. And remember, this isn't school. *Enjoy.*

THE POEMS
[in no particular order]

Muddy Chucks

Soppy shoes run through the field of possibility.
Left, right, left, they pound with electricity.
A petulance to their stride, a wrinkle nowhere in sight.
Their youthful toes awake all of momma's woes,
when the truck daddy bought begins to rust,
and the muddy chucks,
on her favorite rug
run amok.

The children in the field begin their laughter,
while momma looks on, down, and up,
feeling the weight of the oncoming pitter-patter.
The footprints on the porch, imprinted with different
patterns,
all tell the same manner; however,
with the decreasing rains of Saturn,
the water rusts all, leaving all who remain wondering:
did it even matter?

Momma smiles though, watching the children run around.
Even when the mud begins to change its form,
from darker,
to light brown.

Blue Jays

The blue jay is not actually blue;
in fact, it is gray.
A color that defines the medium between night and day.
An idea that gives its virtue to the morning dew.

My soul, in fact, is blue.
Battered by the rains that coalesce my veins.
Tunnels that soon need a drain,
from dark Azul, to the comforting sky
of a silver hue.

'95 Leo*

No Maclaren, just glaring.
Rocking the Dapperton, wondering what's happening.
Pensive to the sight, with childish delight.
To the woman who works behind the camera's moonlight.
Figure I'll pose, for the flower boy who knows—
when it's time to dream, and when it's time to see.

Aperture.
Shutter.
Speed.

*This poem was originally used for an Instagram post during a time when I was a part of a collective. Some of the allusions will be lost amongst a lot of readers, but I just want to clarify that I used a lot of inspiration from Tyler, The Creator's ideas (e.g., *flower boy*). Alas, this poem is deeply personal to me, so forgive a potential lapse in resonance. Oh, and "Dapperton" refers to the artist Gus Dapperton. Google him. Pay attention to his hair. His song "Prune, you talk funny" is really good, too.

Drunk at a Wedding

I went to a friend's wedding today:
a winery, ripe with grapes and grass.
I walked to the groom after the ceremony:
a tall boy, filling up glass.

We drank sangria, watching the sunset over the endless
field;
a few drops fell, spilling onto the golden yield.
We watched on as the drops entered the earth,
solidifying a pact, stronger than birth.

Above, I see birds fly away with grace.
Below—I'll stand a part—
till death fills this pretty place.

Musings of a Genius Child*

They don't believe you **can**
but the only person worth proving is **you**.
Accept the **love**
you harness, and bring it to **an**
understanding, like the **eagle**
in the sky, trying to **tame**
its wings. You must soar above the fear, **or**
ask yourself: do you really wish to stay in the **wild?**

These, my love, are the musings of a genius child.

*This poem was inspired by Terrence Hayes' "The Golden Shovel."
An amazing poem that used Gwendolyn Brooks' "We Real Cool" in a
clever way. Hayes used each word of Brooks' poem to end his lines.
Seriously, go check it out. For my poem I used a line from the late-
great Langston Hughes. I owe him for this one. The bolded words,
read vertically, are an excerpt from his poem "Genius Child."

To My Dear, and Future, Assassin

Your snub-nosed kisses;
your garrote-wire necklace;
your smooth stilettos;
they glide down my spine.

Like Pink Moscato—
a wine—
lying in the hole with you
is such sweet divine.

Expectations

I awake in the misty moonlight,
where spectres guide me to your sight.
I wander through your field,
with yellow petals that erase my shield.

I meet you halfway; where you fill my cup—
WAIT! *What the fuck is this?*—
I don't like 7up.

Amor

Dark, silty, and imbued—
a river runs through—
washing away the stain
of all my dirty pain.

Your fingers pluck the lyre,
and baby, you light my fire.

Bright, clear, and anew—
your words pierce true—
like the arrows of those,
that cleanse my soul.

Bless me, Amor.
Forever,
more.

Urn

My great grandfather's urn.
My grandfather's urn.
My father's urn.

I look at the mantle,
and slowly wipe the dust away.
I look at my son,
and kiss him before work today.

Someday,
he will do the same.
When the porcelain turns to ash,
and his pockets, slowly, fill with cash.

The Cabbie's Realization (The Taxi)

Sometimes,
The Taxi in all of us drives blindly.
To and fro, the people who enter inside,
chew and gnaw wildly.
They feed lust, carnality, and spite,
until the road is empty,
full dark, no clear line of sight.

Sometimes,
we reach certain fares and look often,
at the passengers, we study like the boffin.
The rearview mirror keeps their faces,
yet their hands, thoughts, and hearts
are lost to us; black, vacuous spaces.

Sometimes,
fare, well it is.
And sometimes,
fare, well it is not.

However, most of the time,
The Taxi in all of us drives along.
Even when the roads we take,
and the hands we shake,
are far too often
oblong.

Seasons

Spring—
the buds bloom.
Summer—
the flowers awake.
Fall—
the petals loom.
Winter—
the chrysanthemums wake.

Remember, sweet frown
whether October or June
when the sun is down,
and the seasons anew—
remember—
this rose is for you.

Letting Her Go (Coming Home)

My tires always tread familiar grooves in the driveway
when I go home.
Although, stepping on familial stone, sometimes
my steps feel foreign; alone.

My father moves past me with anger on his brow,
while I look on at my mother,
wiping the windows, whispering wow.

Inside, I ask her what's wrong, but nothing.
It's time for food, nothing more,
nothing to see, except a sea,
one birthed from grease; the other cheese.

I drive away after eating, feeling the bumps in the road,
patches that have long been neglected.
By the mason, and his stone.

I get to my apartment and sit to watch a show,
while I get a call from my mother, waiting for father
to come home.
She talks about her day, while I watch the microwave.
It's okay—I say—letting her go,
knowing full well,
she needs it the most.

Writer Sits at A Coffee Shop with Friend

I let my friend read this poem, and,
well, he told me I needed
structure.

Well,

I told him thank
you. And kept typing
away.

Friend,
the more often we seek validation,
the more weight we put on our middle section.
A pebble that festers, grows to be a boulder.
So, Friend, listen to this advice; it's okay to ignore
even the people in your corner.

The only validation you need is…

…wait…Friend…
…can you repeat what you said?

Grabbing Breakfast with Dad

My father orders a number three: his usual.
Two eggs, two links, and a decaf drink: unusual.

No caffeine, my father tells me.
Afraid of stones, and not the ones that roll.
He eats his sunny sides, while I complete mine.

Looking at my father, wrinkles by his eyes,
I realize; that the hardest part of growing up,
isn't getting old; but instead,
watching the egg from the yoke
—spoil—
a dash of thunder, then ozone.

I pay for my father, who drinks his decaf;
a gentle reminder, that today, or tomorrow,
may be all that we have.

Cracks

I looked at some sidewalk chalk,
and asked my lover what they thought.

They saw a face, while I saw a vase.

Walking away, I see the cracks in our vase,
wherein a flower dries out, and my lover walks
at an unfamiliar pace.

Awake at 1:37 AM

By nine, they go to bed.
By ten, they sit awake instead.
By eleven, dreams lead them to sleep.
By twelve, the nightmares creep.

Awake, the shadows cast their hue
over the arms of a temporal view.
However, this place
a field of electric sheep,
is always the same:
luminous, blue, and sleek.

The LED peers into us, as we gaze past
the entities scrolling towards our feet—
lives of adjacent neighbors in fleet,
all in search of the same raft:

sleep.

Dog in My Rearview Mirror

The stray dog carried on,
following its transient nature.
Like a Ronin—
a mission not set upon.

A journeyman, myself
crosses
the path of the traveler.

I offer the dog a hand,
a pat; a snack.
I even stay awhile,
brushing the earth off its back.

I leave the dog to its devices,
knowing full well its path.
However, I'm taken aback
when I see this lone warrior
running—
towards my back.

Road Trips (Without You)

Not even the blurry tableau
can remove the thought of your shadow.
Not even the shuffle of harmonies
can quiet the sound of your symphonies.
As I lay my head on the glass,
my father drives us past.
It's no place I know,
where I'd have a chance to see your mass.

Because you matter to me, even when
I cannot see a vista of green.
Without you, the car rolls on.
It's a bleak vision.
One so bitter, yet soon to be
my favorite street.

Running from The Past

I saw my ex the other day,
on the run,
but didn't know what to say.

I stood there,
watching their hips sway.
Wondering to myself,
if I should stay.

I thought of turning back.
But instead, I ran past.
The gray clouds behind me
hold tears, spilling glass.

Onto brighter paths, and beautiful stars;
those with illuminating gas.

So hurry, keep running.
Don't let the past catch
you, and ultimately,
strike a match.

The Loin Stone (For Jade)

Somewhere in the darkness, I found
the forest Jade.
Touching, kissing—
I hug the mess I've made.

Awake,
I feel the pain
of my Hera. The shame.
What will I say, to her?
She, who virtues the crane.

Regarding Zeus,
I close my eyes away.
For in my forest's eye:
I search for Jade.

Watching Movies with You

The hardest part of watching movies
with you, is that I fear of what you'll do.

Because I have my fair share of cinematic wounds,
and to show you them scares me.
It's nothing personal, we just aren't that far.

But to explore my favorites with you,
is a re-opening; an insertion
and possibly, a new scar.

So listen, let's just watch some Netflix.
It'll be easier if you decide to leave stage-right
exit.

90 Pounds

At the table I sit.
Two plates, one chance,
don't miss.

I smile, at my partner,
whose gaze fills me
with a feeling,
much softer.

Window eyes that wipe sweat
with each glance.
Dark crystals that shine upon
this heavy dance.

I pick up our plates,
feeling their weight,
and I strain, sensing shame.

But thank God for my partner;
who lifts my pain.
Especially on those days
when I really need
someone stronger.

Sundays

Mother,
forgive me, but I have sinned.
Going to church as a kid was
never the life I wanted to live.

There, I counted the spots in the ceiling,
instead, of listening to the healing.
There, I dismissed hands with strangers,
even when I knew, they weren't the real danger.

Sundays were supposed to be another day,
where a kid could run instead of pray.
Somedays where the weekday would stay away,
and the sun would shine its petulant ray.

However, I felt a familiar shame,
when I went to church today.

Mother,
I'm trying to see it from your perspective,
but with age, I feel perceptive.
That moving forward,
and changing ways,
Sundays,
will never be the same.

Blocks

I **[don't]** want to write this.
Seriously, **[I hate this. stop]**
[okay] you aren't stopping.
I **[don't]** know what you
are trying to prove.
But trust me, it's going
[to flop].

Wait, I kind of liked that.
Okay: let's keep this going.
Maybe I could try this, or—
oh my, this page feels **[flat]**.

Well, let me just keep on
going. If I add an idea—
oh my, that's **[not]** what I want.
I can see the page forming,
and man…if I had stopped?

Wow, I can't believe it,
but I think I'm growing.
[so, listen…delete this]*

*The bracket in English grammar is a tool writers use to add information—normally to quotes—that may require supplemental structure. However, it's important to know that when omitted, the brackets show the original text. Now, maybe you could omit the brackets here; maybe you can see what you've been trying to tell yourself all along. Stay creative, dear reader.

Bonfire

To my dearest friends,
I love you.

Wherever we go,
I want you to know,
that we are linked
by an oath,
stronger than oak.

Brothers are forever.
A flame that lasts
no matter the weather.

To my embers,
I thank you,
for the lights you show me—
brighter
and
higher.

Oh, how I can't wait to retire.
When all of us have lived,
to the degrees that we aspire;
and we can finally sit,
together,
watching our fire.

Alone, Together

I await the day with you,
and, staring at my phone,
I scroll until it's noon.

Soon, you come into my house,
kick off your shoes, settle in,
and dissolve onto your couch.

I talk with you, but listen,
hearing the reflections—
held in your eyes—
slowly glisten.

Although, I wish I felt better.
Even though you are here,
I feel alone,
together.

iPod Shuffle

I want to be
like Kenny G.

Soft tips
Smooth lips
Fingers that caress
Silver pips.

I want to be
like Freddie Mercury.

Loose hips
Silk dips
Cruise ships
Rich sips
Jazzy riffs—

—In velvet blue,
under the moon,
—with you—
I want to be used
like sweaty dance shoes.

Divorced Poet

This is a haiku:
a lyric that bends for you.
Except Jane, fuck you.

Vampire's Reflection

I wash your blood on my face,
and search myself in the mirror,
finding something, less opaque.

I only feed because I have to.
It's a part of my design.
Just like the sharp kisses,
the soft rubs, and even the wine.

Another drip from your cup,
eyes see, as I grip your spine,
filling up mine.

In the mirror;
the red face before me floats.
It tells a story of the creature,
the one who kept feeding—
a diet consisting of hopes.

Coffee Shop Zombie (Choosing Monsters)

To those afraid of the coffee shop zombie:
don't be. There is no need to flee.

Drop your shotgun. Drop your hammer.
There is no reason to stammer.

It only wants your brain;
your synaptic space.
Now, doesn't that sound great?

No? Well, good luck then
with your nightclub wolf.
He, who feeds, by the west end wharf.

The one who stares
at your hair,
dreaming of his snare.

While the coffee shop zombie lingers,
on the thought you brewed,
over hot coffee, and guitar fingers
in tune.

Kid Atlas

The clock ticks its timeless rhyme,
against the shifting, harsh hands of mine.

As weight is put upon me,
I hear my inner child crying
of a moment, in time,
where the adults aren't fighting.

Alas,
Atlas shrugs on his recliner,
while I hold everything up
aghast,
waiting for your hands
to lift our world—higher.

Taking Off

My eyes roll back;
my heart goes flat;
my feet begin to sink;
and then again, all I can think:

taking off with you
makes me feel brand new.

High and by,
floating in the sky
I look through your window
and place my resting head
on a beautiful, pink pillow.

My First Uber Driver

His name was Julio.

A driver, heading elsewhere.
A father, blessing everywhere.

His name was Julio.

Who carried a lesson
which traveled thirty years
through blood, sweat—
smudged mirrors.

His name was Julio.

Who called life the beautiful struggle;
a constant battle, between foes,
who so desperately seek solace
under cover—with entwined toes.

His name was Julio.

A transient survivor.
My first Uber driver.

Drunk

It comes in waves,
of others, of spirits,
of drowned colors.

Neon pink/baby blue shells,
purple rocks; magenta salt.
Balancing the crystal dunes,
the water calls out.

I listen to the shore,
holding my glass oar.
I look at the pretty sea
who winks, another pour?

I wade, wade, and wade;
an olive dipped in salt;
I soon fade, fade, and fade:
a curtain, pulled back
no applause.

The Moon King

Between two soft palms
The Moon King dips his toes
as the sun bath calms.

An alabaster soul—caught
off guard by the mold;
a warmth that holds
much more than he thought.

The Moon King lowers his crown,
placing his face, within, the liquid ground.
Becoming one—
with the father;
the mother;
—and The Sun.

In Domino Park

Elderly fingers click and clack
of long-ago diplomatic talks.
While younger faces snack
on the foods of various walks.

Pieces connect over coffee,
building onto each other
like smoke on skin
of a fine cigar.
Rolled by nations,
seeking the refuge
of a smile in the dark.
Illuminated, by my time
in Domino Park.

Where the tomb holds flowers,
for the people, who withstood
the boneyards; the hours.

Hotel Sex (The Morning After)

Sweet, is the sound of your laughter.
Sweet, is the morning after.
When your nape, and my palm,
checkout one: a rusted; yet silver
platter.

Eventually

Restless legs,
broken pegs,
they teach me to rest.

Hollow room,
arrested bloom,
I worry about our test.

I run through a guide,
with you by my side
and suddenly
the feelings subside.

I let the markings go,
don't look back;
and keep running
full stride.

Eventually, I will pass.
You, and I, will stay moving.
Far until,
my lungs,
collapse.

Cupid's Bruise

Heavy wings fall on fibrous strings,
while cherubim eyes look on,
high above, the mezzanine.

Two friends shoot their shot
at a skewed target.
While two lovers talk,
adjacent, and a part.

All aim their tips,
while cupid is affixed.
Not on their accuracy,
but by the purple—
below his own lips.

Arrows cross the meridian
while Cupid sits alone,
covering his bruise;
one, out of a million.

Angry Orchards

Past the angry orchard,
I lay in my tame garden.
And through its glower,
I now understand the pain
of the flower.

Who watches
me tend to my buds.
While the orchard,
a heavy son,
waits for his;

a river,
that runs.

The Trio of Leaves

Three vagabonds listlessly wandered
rolling rocks and milling high.
This strange tableau of souls pondered
measuring cocks, but asking why?

The dreamer;
lost in the stem
brings the sweetener.

The poet;
lost in the soil
begins to sow it.

And the vision;
lost in the root
solidifies the mission.

Three buds, from the same plant,
begin to sprout.
Full bloom, no moon,
their transition is paramount.

From a bundle of petals,
to a trio of leaves,
the wind blows,
but the endless summer keeps.

Concrete Feet

My timid feet,
stay off the street.
This retreat,
is due to much more
than the summer heat.

I stay on the blade
that cuts straight.
A minor pain,
never early,
but far, too late.

I travel to the curb,
edging my feet.
Someday, I say,
it'll work,
with my feet,
on the concrete.

Semi

Outside me:
She drives
a light freight.

Inside me:
She supplies
a heavy weight.

The semi of my dreams rides on
despite the extended thumb,
of a sojourn mourn,
from a torn,
omnibus.

Modern Romance

It is better to be dead,
than to be left,
on read.

Leaving Metropolis

The place of your hold,
is set upon my shoulder.
The weight of your world,
is vast, much warmer.

Window eyes watch me in flight,
as I fly away, to a lane,
much colder.

Couch Co-Op

Player zero has entered the game.
And pretty soon, he will complain.
Not because of the onslaught,
brought on by the robots,
but,
by the players to his left, those
—*reloading!*—incendiary shots.

The burns coalesce the soul,
even though, my own bro,
doesn't know.

That he controls my player;
he, my hidden slayer.

Ozymandias' Echo Chamber

The cracks of my stone
are a product of my design;
a cry for a tone
for a failure of mine.

Ancient travelers dwell
in the freshness of my hell.
An echo from a shell,
married with, a bell.

I await in my chamber;
until the sand
meets the paper.

I await in my chamber
for the suture
of a statue's future.

The Purple Loofa

I stare at the purple loofa
which hangs loosely on my shower wall.
I remember the way it felt
washing with, and without, your beige hall.

Time has come and gone
and the shower head has stopped;
however, the water will flow—
anon and on.

Loud Places

The rest is noise,
but with you,
there is music.

The Tiger

Class,
you are dismissed.

You walk out the door, looking up
to see the darkness surrounding you.
You tread lightly to your car
aware of the icy path in front of you.
At home, you throw the backpack down
anxious to pick it back up.

At your desk, you smile
briefly
thinking
of your coronation:
the black and yellow crown,
the pendulous tassel,
the adulation of peers.
In bed, you hide beneath
false security, blankets of tears.

You await the tranquility
of eight, seven, six, five, four,
hours before it begins again.
Gazing at the white, clinical ceiling
you see a movement in the periphery.

You take a peek, thinking of childhood
and see The Tiger. Its fangs red
like roses, white

death becomes its form.

Paralysis seeps into your veins
rendering you like the gazelle,
carrion.
And keep calm
you say, to subside the feeling,
but claws impress upon your bed,
each movement causing a wave,
a shift
to that final resting place.

Dreaming, lucidity takes reign
and you find yourself in your kingdom
moving, managing, and molding.
You see your subjects sitting by your side,
respecting the wisdom you impart.
Some challenges arise, but you
are capable.
You roar.

You awake.

The Tiger looks into you,
waiting for your final breath.
You look back, conquering white death.
Feeling the strength,
feeling your voice,
you look back, and command the request.
Tiger,
you are dismissed.

You get out of bed, looking up
to see the light in your windows.
You tread lightly to your car
noting the beautiful dew on petals—
those—
of ever-changing willows.

Toxic

Open up my arms
so I can let you go.

It's hard to say goodbye,
but easy to say hello.

So make sure and leave me,
in the morning,
before the radiation glows.

Elsewhere

Wherever you fly,
make it elsewhere.
Don't settle for the island,
in the middle of nowhere
or somewhere.

Center yourself,
elsewhere.

Where the seasons,
give us reasons,
to catch air.

Mrs. Blue Bird

Blessed,
on my shoulder,
the blue bird rests
soft, selfless hands,
that cleanse my chest.

Now,
I hear the sound
of your heavenly tune
that enters, that fills
my favorite room.

Soon,
the indigo whispers
of a grandmother's tune:
bring a sweet cadence,
of time, of love,
anywhere; renewed.

The Junkie's Scrapbook

The cellophane days,
of a high time,
open up inside
the sweet rhyme
of pantomime.

Where the memories retreat,
close to the button;
yet far, from delete.

THE STORIES
[in some particular order]

Author's Note: "<<" is the symbol for rewind and ">>" is the symbol for fast forward. Think of a VCR Player. Remember VHS?

The Blue Beetle

I.

The lonely man clenched his fists on his steering wheel as he watched the girl in red enter her car. She drove a Honda Accord: it was white, dated, and had rust poking out from the bottom of its frame. *A peculiar car for a woman of such looks*, the lonely man thought to himself. He figured younger girls nowadays drove things deemed sporty, flashy, or cute. However, this car wasn't cute. It was ugly to the lonely man. *An odd mix*, he thought to himself as he started his own 4,000-pound sleeping dragon.

The lonely man's car—a utility SUV—awoke, and its blue headlights penetrated the darkness. He watched the girl in red drive on—creating some distance—before downshifting his automatic shifter into *D*.

The roads were empty tonight. *Unusual for a Friday*, he mused.

The girl in red's Honda drove down the road as the lonely man kept its shape in his vision. He always knew when to speed up or slow down when it came to tailing someone.

And as for tonight, the lonely man knew to hang in the periphery: a place he knew far too well.

Moving his gaze from the Honda's taillights in the distance, the lonely man looked in his rearview mirror. And despite his car's dark interior, he regarded his eyes—two islands—and found himself in an ocean of blinding nostalgia. His thoughts galvanized the memory of his childhood.

And as the lonely man returned his vision back to the Honda, spotting a solitary deer on the side of the road for a moment, he couldn't help—hands clutching the steering wheel—but think of Georgia.

<<

"Why are you following me?"

The lonely kid looked to his shoes, avoiding his accuser's face. He wished she would just run away like all the others.

"Hey!"

He waited for her to shove him.

"Look at me."

The lonely kid finally raised his eyes and met hers.

Her sharp, little beads of green pierced the lonely kid inside. The vulnerability he felt in her jade spotlights was unlike any other feeling in the world. Never before had anyone confronted him about his following. All the other girls were too scared to stay—each of them running wild in their colorful summer dresses.

However, the heat from this hot summer day was nothing compared to the heat emanating off Georgia Hadley's brow as she glowered at the lonely kid.

"What are you?" Georgia asked him.

The lonely kid looked at her with tears in his eyes. And for the life of him, he didn't know how to answer that question.

>>

The girl in red's Honda Accord slowly rolled to a stop outside a desolate convenience store. And parked across the street—blue headlights off—the lonely man watched as the girl opened her car door, slowly exiting into the emptiness of night. As he watched her, he noted her beauty. The girl in red had long, dark hair; dreamy, green eyes; and tall, skinny legs.

The lonely man's hands trembled on the wheel as the girl walked inside the convenience store.

<<

"Why are you staring at me?" Georgia whispered.

"Because I like you," the lonely kid said.

"No, you don't. You just like my butt," she whispered.

The lonely kid smiled, looking around the public library. Everyone in sight focused elsewhere. Most read their newly-rented books while others studied. He spotted a few vagrants as well sleeping on a wooden bench near the water fountains. They seemed content to him. And seated next to Georgia, he felt a similar feeling.

The lonely kid smiled. "You don't have a butt."

Georgia laughed loudly.

Heads, of all ages, turned to non-verbally scold the pair. Even the sleeping vagrants began to stir. The lonely kid blushed at all the attention—sinking in his own chair.

"What?" the lonely kid whispered.

"You're funny," she said.

And for the next few weeks, Georgia and the lonely kid were inseparable. Many of the other boys at school even teased him for having a new girlfriend. One boy in particular, Johnny, always gave him the hardest time.

One day, after gym class, Johnny and his followers— more so disciples—circled the lonely kid by his locker. He felt dwarfed by their size. Their larger frames. And panicked, the lonely kid did his best to find a hole to run through. With each attempt out of the human bush, he continued to stay tangled. One boy, Harry, grabbed him by the right arm. And instinctively, the lonely kid struck Johnny's disciple with his left hand. Harry moaned, hands on his nose, and took a few careless steps back like a wounded boxer.

Shocked by his own gumption, noting his shaking fist which hurt, the lonely kid began to cry.

"I think he broke Harry's nose," another Johnny disciple said.

And before anything else could be registered about Harry's nose, Johnny grabbed the lonely kid by his shoulders and shoved him hard against the lockers. The pain in the lonely kid's back shot up to his head like a busted fire hydrant. But luckily, nothing spilled from his mouth.

"You done fighting, faggot?" Johnny asked, tightening his grip on the lonely kid's shoulders.

"Come on, Johnny," another disciple chimed in, "give him one for Harry."

"Yeah," Harry mumbled.

"Fuck Harry," Johnny said. "This one's for his little bitch. What's her name?"

The lonely kid wished to stab Johnny in the eye with a steak knife. He could imagine it, too. It was silver with a white, wooden handle. His mother always kept it hidden in a drawer under some newspaper in their kitchen. She hated the idea of having something lethal in plain sight. It wasn't until she cooked his father a meal that she would bring it out. The lonely kid wondered if she hid it due to their mutual fear of father's drunken results; the crumpled beer cans on the floor; the purple bruises covered up with foundation; or, the subtle—yet lingering—taste of saline.

The lonely kid could see a tear rolling down his cheek in his peripheral vision.

"What are you crying for, you faggot?" Johnny asked. "Is this why Georgia likes you? You cry for her you big fag?"

"I'm not a faggot," the lonely kid whispered.

"*Wha?*" Johnny asked, digging his claws deeper into the lonely kid's shoulders. "You're not a what?"

"I am not a faggot!" the lonely kid screamed, ripping Johnny's hands off of him.

The nearby disciples stepped back with caution. Johnny himself, rubbing his hands, did the same.

Something primal had entered this locker room.

Johnny watched the lonely kid huff and puff, his chest rising up and down like a pneumatic press. There was a wildness in the lonely kid's eyes.

A tempestuous rage.

An absolute anger.

Annihilation.

The lonely kid looked deep into Johnny's eyes.

"If you ever mention Georgia's name again, Johnny," the lonely kid said, "I'll kill your stupid, diabetic brother. I'll creep into your home at night and slit his dumb, little throat with a steak knife."

The lonely kid moved his predatory gaze from Johnny to his disciples behind him.

"The same goes for you all, too. I know your sisters. I've followed them all home. Now, don't make me finish what I started, Harry."

Harry gulped.

And for the first time ever, the lonely kid saw a new shade of color on Johnny's face.

It was the color of pale terror.

The lonely kid laughed, rubbing his left fist.

"What are you?" Johnny asked.

A cold silence floated throughout the locker room. And finally, the lonely kid smiled to Johnny, thinking of the perfect response.

II.

"Your total is 5.47," Ben said, placing a pack of cigarettes in a plastic sack.

The girl in red looked in her wallet.

To Ben, noting the cigarette brand, there really was no use in buying the high-end stuff. *A cigarette was a cigarette*. It didn't matter if it was gold-plated or scraped out of an ashtray; the end result would always be the same. He thought back to his freshman year biology class as he finished checking this girl out, remembering the time his teacher brought out the lung of a smoker. How black and amorphous it looked to him that day.

How alien.

The girl in red thanked Ben—a polite gesture he seldom heard these days—and headed for the door. Although, turning around to him once again—reminding him of an old detective show that hung on that balance of "just one more thing"—she looked towards a rotating kiosk near the register. She craned her neck and reached into her pocket. The change inside her jeans danced around her knuckles and into Ben's ears. He watched her dig for the spare coinage—noting her attractiveness.

As the girl in red brushed her hair back, selected a keychain from the rotating kiosk, and placed it on the counter, Ben felt his skin warm. He was never any good at small talk, and regarding this girl—and his recent break-up—he figured he could try to be.

Quite ironic, Ben thought, considering his current profession of customer service. However, propelled by some feeling, he pushed on to fight his inherent reticence.

"Good choice," Ben said.

He picked up the keychain, studying its grooves.

"Volkswagen."

"Excuse me," the girl in red said.

"*Volkswagen*," he said, pointing to the keychain. "It's a blue Volkswagen Beetle."

"Oh," she said, taking a closer look at the keychain. "Yeah. Thanks."

Ben shook his head, hating himself for being that guy who overstated the obvious.

"No problem," he said, keeping his flushed vision on the register.

Ben rung up the keychain, accepted her spare change, finished the transaction, and watched her receipt roll out of a nearby machine.

"Would you like a bag?" Ben asked.

She laughed. "No, that's fine. Thank you though. That's very sweet."

Ben's cheeks turned a subtle shade of red as he handed her the keychain. "No worries. Have a good night."

The girl in red nodded to him and walked away. He studied the curls that formed at the base of her hair that bounced with each step she took. And overhead, before she was out of the store for good—*perhaps forever*—the store's audio system transformed the music to one of his favorite songs.

Ben smiled.

And just before exiting, once again, the girl in red stopped at another kiosk. On display, she regarded her reflection in a variety of multi-colored sunglasses. Ben wondered if she was lingering on purpose. Perhaps, he thought rather creatively, she was a fugitive on the run, crafting a new fashion sense as she traveled state-to-state...store-to-store. A pair of glasses, along with the keychain, being the final touches of some new persona.

Ben smiled again, shaking his head.

As the girl looked for the right pair of glasses, Ben noticed her swaying to the overhead music; he watched her denim hips move to the beat of the song.

And to Ben, the sight was graceful.

Watching her dance, Ben thought of the wheat fields from his childhood. Those warm afternoons on his grandfather's farm where he listened to his elder speak of a past he would never fully understand. Tales surrounded by the swaying stalks of wheat. Tranquil, peaceful, and cozy. Ben often missed that time in his life. At nights, he sometimes thought of the dancing wheat to help him sleep.

"You like the music?" Ben asked.

"Yeah. It's nice. Who is this?"

"It's this cool band *LCD Soundsystem*," Ben started. "Their front man, James Murphy, is a musical genius. The way he blends and layers his music. It's amazing."

The girl in red giggled as she placed a pair of blue-tinted shades back on the kiosk; they hung askew.

"Are you a music critic or something?" she asked.

"No, *sadly*. I go to State. I'm studying education. I'm going to be English Teacher someday. Someday soon."

"English?" she asked.

"Yeah, I like to read and write. Figured teaching was the best route to take in the field. I have hopes of publishing something one day. Although, like my father always said: Plan B isn't just for girls."

The girl in red laughed loudly.

Ben flushed.

He felt the pleasant shift in their conversation and felt better about his small talk abilities. The thought of asking for her number jumped out to him, but he figured he should tread lightly. He did in fact just meet this girl.

However, strangely enough, Ben felt that he'd heard her laugh his entire life. Maybe it was just the helpless romance cajoling his heart, but nonetheless, he was sure this moment meant something.

It had to, right?

This girl, in her red jacket, was special to Ben. It was a feeling that gave feet to his words.

"What's your name?" he asked.

The girl in red looked up, meeting his gaze. The redness in her cheeks warmed Ben's skin further.

"Kayla."

"Kayla," he repeated.

"What's yours?" she asked.

"Ben."

"Hello, Ben."

"Hello."

They stared at each other smiling for some time. Overhead, the sounds of LCD Soundsystem finished, and a new song begun. And not too long after, the overhead sound of a *ding* broke their spell.

A large man, sniffling with a handful of Kleenex, entered the convenience store. The portent man rushed for the restroom. And Ben could tell this man would offer it no mercy. Working in convenience, Ben knew the literal shitshow he signed up for. However, despite the fecal downside of his job, he was glad he worked this Friday night. Ben was glad to have met Kayla. He knew he would replay the scene later in his mind like a movie.

"Have a goodnight, Ben," Kayla said, walking away, "I'll see you around."

"Take care."

Kayla smiled, turning her frame to the door. Ben watched her exit with her sack of smokes and her keychain.

Ding.

In the store alone, except for the large man in the restroom, Ben figured the smokes weren't for her. Working at this store for the last several months, he always knew how to spot the non-smokers. It wasn't just their body language. It was often the question: "what do you mean by shorts?"

Ben chuckled, unsure of his amateur deduction skills, and found his eyes on another reason to see Kayla again.

He stared at her receipt.

Here we go, Ben thought, ripping the receipt.

Outside, Ben watched Kayla opening her car door. And for some reason, he imagined her driving something else.

"Hey," Ben called out.

Kayla looked at Ben and smiled.

"Yes?" she asked.

Ben walked the distance of the parking lot to her Honda and held out his hand.

"Don't forget your receipt."

Kayla stared at the little paper intently; her smile remained consistent.

Ben chuckled, waiting for her to take it from him.

"Thanks," she said, taking the receipt and slipping it into her jeans, "you really are a gentleman."

Ben watched Kayla enter her car, and he was struck by sadness. He realized that she would be off having a night—doing whatever—while he was stuck cleaning toilets and stocking overpriced bottles of water.

Her Honda pulled out of the parking lot and headed south.

Downtown.

Kayla might not have been a smoker, Ben thought, but she could have been a clubber. As his eyes shifted from her fading taillights, another set of lights caught Ben's line of sight. Parked across the street—floating in the empty parking lot of Benchley's Grocery—blue headlights spotlighted him. Ben had to shield his eyes due to their brightness. And shortly after, the blue headlights panned left, heading southbound as well.

Ben stared out watching the diminishing SUV head in the direction of Kayla until its blue lights became one with the overwhelming darkness.

In the empty parking lot, noting the low hum of artificial lighting, Ben sighed.

And as he walked back to the store, the large man from before walked out.

Ding.

Before his journey elsewhere, the large man regarded Ben and nodded to him solemnly.

"Sorry, brother," the large man said.

"For what?" Ben asked.

The large man kept walking. "I'm sorry."

Later on, finally summoning the courage to enter the men's restroom, Ben understood why the large man was apologetic.

Ding.

Ben looked at the mop bucket in the corner of the restroom, stomaching the smell, and realized some people really are animals.

Ding.

Some people really are filthy creatures.

Ding.

III.

The lonely kid watched Georgia as she threw rocks into the river behind her house. It was something she loved to do. He loved the way she fastidiously picked the rocks for throwing. How careful and methodical she was when analyzing the curvature, shape, and density of a stone.

For many nights, the lonely kid lay in bed thinking about those rocks. The thought of something so inherently hard being transformed, in her hands, into something so soft never left him.

The lonely kid loved Georgia.

He watched her pick up a smooth stone near the river's edge.

And like a painter admiring their work, Georgia smiled and readied her form.

Many times, regarding stone throwing, she instructed the lonely kid to always keep his back straight, keep his elbows tight to his ribs, and pray.

The last rule always tickled him. The lonely kid wasn't religious by any means, but he respected her conviction.

The lonely kid's parents weren't religious either. In fact, they weren't even the standard, Sunday Christians that plagued most suburban neighborhoods. His parents prayed, but only when it was convenient. The only time any sense of metaphysical protection was given to him was usually from behind a locked bathroom door; his father panting on the other side with a beer in one hand and a weathered belt in the other. And even during those dark times in the bathroom, waiting for father to roll over, he never joined in with his mother's holy murmurings.

However, watching Georgia—dressed in her turquoise dress with a red bow in her dark hair—he conceded to the notion of a higher power.

Georgia threw the stone across the river; it danced a few beats before finally ceasing its rhythm.

"Do you know how to pray?" Georgia asked, watching the stone's ripples in the river.

"I think so," the lonely kid said, clapping his hands together, "something like this, right?"

"No, silly," she turned to him. "You don't need to put your hands together to pray. That's just what they do at church."

"But my mom does it."

"Oh," Georgia said, feeling the conviction in his words. "Well, if that's how *you* begin, then that's how *we'll* begin. Come on."

Georgia led him to the edge of the river.

"Sit with me," she said, rubbing his elbow.

As Georgia settled herself near the river's edge, sand and dirt caking the bottom of her dress, she tugged at his cotton pants.

"Come on," Georgia said with a smile.

The lonely kid sighed and began to sit. He kept his gaze on the flowing river in front of him; the murky stream abstracted small torpedoes of life that wiggled within. He figured the moving shadows must have been minnows swimming home. He had seen them here once before.

Georgia shuffled around and sat in front of him with her legs crossed. They stared at each other for a while. Rhythmic claps of water gently brushed against one another as she lifted her hands in genuflection. The sight of her hands together made the lonely kid think of home.

The blows against the bathroom door.

The incoherent pleas to God.

His trembling, interlocked fingers.

"Are you okay?" she asked.

"Yeah," he responded. "Just wish I didn't have to go home. Wish I was like these minnows here. Wish I had a place to swim to."

Georgia looked at him quizzically.

She scooted next to him and pointed to the water. The lonely kid followed her finger, watching the silted minnows ebb to the surface of the river for a moment of clarity. Their silver, reflective scales shimmered across the water like the sun's reflection at sunset.

"You think those minnows have a special home?" she asked.

"Yeah," he said, turning to her. "Probably a nice one with a warm bed, too."

Georgia smiled. "You don't honestly expect me to explain why that's impossible?"

"I know," he said.

"You do?"

"Yeah."

"Well, I don't," she said. "Why don't you tell me what's wrong?"

The lonely kid looked at her with eyes holding back impending rivulets of salt.

"Why don't you want to go home?" she asked, touching his shoulder.

"Drop it," he said to her. "I don't want to talk about it."

Georgia pulled back her hand, moving her eyes to the flowing stream.

Overhead, the leaves rustled against one another; a cold wind formed by the river.

"Okay," she said. "I'll drop it."

The lonely kid wiped at his eyes. He expected to feel tears.

"Thank you," he said.

"Of course," she said. "I'm here for you."

Georgia placed her hand on his thigh and the lonely kid stared at it. Looking at her soft hand, he was reminded of the rocks she threw.

The stones.

The lonely kid imagined Georgia picking him up in both of her soft hands—studying him—and tossing him across the river to the other side.

The other side.

A place, to the lonely kid, with no pain.

A place of love.

A paradise.

Although, regarding the river's distance, the lonely kid figured he would never make it to the other side.

The lonely kid figured he would sink halfway across the river, the shape and color of his body merging with the murky darkness.

Remembering to breathe, the lonely kid moved Georgia's hand away from his thigh and lifted his knees to his chest. Georgia sat there looking at him. Her gaze felt immense on his skin. He glanced at her in his periphery—noticing that same quizzical expression on her face from before.

"Why do you do it?" she asked.

The lonely kid stared at the minnows.

"Do what?"

"Why do you follow people? Why did you follow me?"

The lonely kid's focus intensified on the river. He wished he could pierce through the muddy water and find the minnow home he fancied.

"You know," he began, "maybe you're right."

"About what?"

"About what you said earlier," he said. "About the minnows and their home."

Georgia stared at him, her eyes drawing a blank.

"What are you talking about?" she asked.

"Maybe," he begun, "the minnows don't have a special place to go. Somewhere specific. What if—*just if*—these minnows aren't searching for a home. What if all those little fish are just riding from one point to another, following the current to a new situation. An escape from their past. *This* moment in *this* stream," he continued, placing his hand into the river, watching the brown water flow across his knuckles, "what if this spot in the stream is just like many other spots before. What if we're like the fish in the river? What if we never have a home to rest, but just keep going? *Spot to spot.* Moment to moment."

The lonely kid looked across the river. "What if our purpose is to never stop moving, Georgia? To never stop following the next situation."

Georgia stared at him blankly. He regarded her eyes cautiously.

"Am I making any sense to you?" he asked her, withdrawing his hand from the stream.

She kept staring at him with no real expression.

"Georgia?"

The cold wind that filtered near the river let up, releasing a warmth that washed over Georgia as she let out a small smile.

The lonely kid fixated on it.

"You're weird," Georgia said.

The lonely kid smiled. "You're weird."

"No."

"Yes," he said.

"Maybe."

Above them, the leaves in the trees rustled once more, sending birds into the sky. Tiny shadows of movement scattered across the lonely kid's face as he looked up. He watched the birds, which looked like coots to him, soar high against the sun.

"So," Georgia began, "am I...your next situation?"

"No," he said, swallowing air, "my only."

The lonely kid leaned over and kissed Georgia on her lips. Startled, she pulled away with roses painted on her cheeks. And looking at her flushed skin, he felt the urge to apologize. He would've done it, too. He would've done it, gone home, and let sleep bring on the next day. He would've found his next situation somehow. There were plenty of other girls he could follow. He would've kept going along like the minnows...he would've—

Georgia grabbed the lonely kid's face and pulled him close. Their lips connected with mature intensity. There was so much force between them that their passion toppled them into the river.

Splash!

They flowed and laughed together, alongside the minnows, to the next spot in the stream of time.

IV.

On the road, Kayla opened her glovebox of mementos and placed the blue beetle keychain inside.

And near the keychain, Kayla noticed the cheap lighter her ex-boyfriend gave to her some months ago. The lighter was ornamented with pink seashells. The sight of it brought back memories of her and her ex walking along the beaches of Texas. Months ago, before the end, they had driven down to Galveston for a weekend away and spent a lot of their time by the shore. And watching the ocean surf, pondering life's important questions—*do you think nostalgia has a smell?*—they shared cigarettes.

And in retrospect, digging out the sordid relic covered in seashells, Kayla realized she only smoked to build some tenuous solidarity between them.

Kayla chuckled, rolling her window down.

And as the glass lowered, giving room for fresh air to enter her Honda, Kayla also remembered how the moonlight casted a blue hue on that shore in Galveston; the sand becoming blue. The sight looked futuristic to her. It was like something out of a Ray Bradbury story she had read as a child.

The future, Kayla thought, throwing her ex's lighter out the window, listening to it clink as it kissed the road.

The future.

This was something Kayla often thought about on the drives back to her father's house.

Sunny beaches, skimpy swimwear, and solace.

Kayla wanted to become an actress in Hollywood.

And on these drives, more so errands for her father's smoking addiction, she contemplated a path in doing so.

Kayla figured she could save up enough for the initial move out there with her friend, Iris. She already had about a grand saved up from her job bartending, but she knew she would need at least another couple hundred for the deposit once they got there. Kayla and her friend planned on sharing a one-bedroom apartment. And while there, in the land of H-O-L-L-Y-W-O-O-D, the duo figured they could work restaurant gigs to stay afloat in the interim between their auditions. Their tips alone at work, at least for Kayla, brought no hesitation in the dreamy pursuit. As well, Kayla knew she was cute enough to get hired for her looks alone. And having everything seemingly planned out, regarding the pop-cultural paradigm, she figured she would have to pay her dues as some extra in a rapper's music video to get the ball rolling for her *serious* career.

Kayla tried to think of a current rapper's name. She placed the words "young" and "little" with an assortment of household objects and laughed. As well, she reckoned all the greats working today had to start somewhere.

Kayla thought of a Juicy Fruit commercial starring Brad Pitt as she continued home.

The Midwest was no place for dreams, Kayla thought. Instead, the gilded fields of Los Angeles were the perfect place for a budding flower with ambition to blossom.

Kayla was willing to do almost anything for her chance to make it big.

However, Kayla knew for certain she would never find herself ass backwards on a leather couch.

She had dignity.

She knew well enough to never drop to her knees for anybody else but God. And as Kayla thought of church, a notion she hadn't entertained for a long time, she reached into her jeans for her phone and dialed her friend, Iris.

And three rings later, Iris picked up.

"Hey girl," Iris said. "What are you up to?"

"Just heading back from the store. Dad needed his smokes. What are you up to?"

"You're still his errand girl, aren't ya?"

"Don't be a bitch," Kayla said.

Iris made a guttural noise into the phone. The noise reminded Kayla of the sound posh, middle-aged women made at risqué jokes.

"Somebody's time of the month is here," Iris said.

Kayla hated how comfortably rude Iris was. She figured Hollywood would be a perfect fit for her: the land of bluntness.

"Hello?" Iris asked. "You there, girl?"

Kayla zoned out, thinking of the future.

She had many dreams of heading into an audition. Kayla envisioned the porcelain floor of a casting agency, pockmarked with the small grooves of many high heels of aspiring actresses. Heels coming and going. Heels heading into the promise land, and others heading back to their Midwestern exile.

And in these dreams, Kayla would eventually make it to a white room where an old woman resided. The woman wore massive bifocals and had outrageous, blonde hair. The woman would judge her, giving Kayla 30 seconds to make an impression.

The time allotted would feel like an eternity. And after Kayla was done, the woman would gaze into her soul with her grandiose optics. The woman would then open her mouth, and before the verdict, Kayla would awake.

She always awoke before her judgment.

This habitual dream kept the idea of Hollywood buoyant for Kayla. She needed to hear what the woman really had to say.

The absence of this knowledge burned a hole into her soul daily.

Iris's voice echoed from the speakerphone, breaking Kayla's trance.

"Hello?"

"I'm here," Kayla said, watching the lines in the middle of the road disappear as she carried along. "How much did you make this week?"

"I made about three hundred. Slow week. What about you?"

Kayla looked into her rearview mirror and noticed two bright lights shining from the distance. These lights didn't belong to the usual sedan, she studied, but something more official. She figured the lights were halogen, given the glow. A piece of information she picked up driving around with her father at night. And as the oncoming vehicle bridged the distance, getting a little too close, the blue headlights lit her up, each beam sending an uncomfortable sensation across her shoulders and neck. The blue glow from the headlights reminded her of the moonlit sand in Galveston.

"Hold on, Iris," Kayla said. "Some dickhead is riding my ass."

"Oh?" Iris asked. "I can call back later if you're busy?"

"Jesus, Iris," Kayla said, waving the car to go around.

The SUV obliged.

Kayla watched as the SUV passed her. She looked to the car's roof and squinted to see if it was a cop.

No lights.

The SUV drove on.

"Kayla?" Iris asked.

"Sorry," she said. "Anyways…what were we talking about?"

"How much did you make this week?" Iris asked.

Kayla told her.

Iris laughed.

"Okay, girl," Iris said. "We might just have to start stripping at this point."

"No way," Kayla said.

"Why not?" Iris asked. "It's not like you have a man telling you not to."

Kayla chuckled, thinking about the cashier she met earlier tonight.

What was his name again?

"Hey," Kayla said.

"What?"

"I met this cute boy tonight."

"What's his name?" Iris asked.

V.

"He's not that cute, Georgia."

"I think he's handsome," Georgia said.

Georgia sat next to her friend, Lydia, watching the lonely kid from afar playing marbles with some other kids. From time to time, with the micro-explosions of colliding glass filling the space between them, the lonely kid looked to her and smiled.

Georgia smiled back.

"You two are something else," Lydia said.

And as the lonely kid looked to her, his attention was cut short by a nearby marble player, a fat boy with ginger hair and buckteeth.

Randall.

What a creep, Georgia thought.

Lydia fixed her dress. "I can't believe out of all the boys you've settled for that one. You do know he's crazy, right?"

"He's crazy about me," Georgia said.

Lydia opened her eyes wide with incredulity.

"No," Lydia said. "He's crazy in the sense that he follows girls."

Georgia kept her gaze fixed on the lonely kid as he shot his small, glass planets into others. She could see a smile on his face as he focused on the game. She wondered if she was still on his mind. *No doubt*, she thought, closing her eyes, and relishing the sweet air of summer.

"He's not following anyone else anymore, Lydia," Georgia said. "He's with me."

Georgia opened her eyes and gave her friend a precocious look. The look of an assured woman.

"Whatever you say, Georgia," Lydia said, looking to the grass. "You can have him."

"And I intend to," she said, looking back to her favorite marble player.

And as she settled her eyes back on the game ahead, a white spotlight shot its way into Georgia's heart as she saw the lonely kid staring at her. His smile elucidated a complexity of feelings. She couldn't help but feel love for him, even at this age. Georgia never fully understood the idea of sex, hearing about it once, but she knew the feelings she felt at nights were the onset of a budding maturity.

Georgia sighed deeply.

Lydia stared at a ladybug.

"What do you know about sex, Lydia?"

"What?" Lydia screamed. "You're not going to have sex with him, right?"

"Hush," Georgia said, patting her friend on the thigh, "never mind."

And with that, Georgia smiled on—relishing the sound of two marbles colliding. Two glass stones rounding off into each other's gravitational pull.

* * *

Clack!

Randall looked over his shoulder to the girls sitting across the street and chortled. The lonely kid couldn't help but see the immaturity in Randall's small, beady eyes when his vision returned. To the lonely kid, the fat boy wore a pair of eyes that would never fully mature due to their light-brown color.

Randall jangled a handful of marbles.

"Well," Randall began, jangling the glass orbs with no rhythm, "what's the next move, kid?"

"I don't know, Randall. I think it's actually your turn."

Randall snickered. "That's not what I'm talking about, man."

Randall gestured his eyes towards the girls, who at this point were leaving.

"That move," Randall said, dropping his marbles onto the ground.

The lonely kid watched Georgia walk away with her friend. He waited for her—holding his gaze—to turn back.

Just a glimpse.

One more for the road.

The lonely kid watched Georgia walk alongside a corner store, her right side bumping lazily into the red brick wall as she furthered her distance. And just before turning the corner of the store, in the direction of home, she looked back to him and smiled.

The lonely kid chuckled, feeling the cool breeze of summer hug him under his armpits. It was a gentle breeze that would carry him home on cupid's wings.

It was a breeze he would never forget.

"Hey!" Randall shouted.

The lonely kid looked at Randall.

"Well?" Randall asked. "When's the wedding?"

The lonely kid sighed, looking at his marbles, and told him.

Randall spent the next five minutes listening. And as the lonely kid talked, with a mature certainty to his words, he reckoned he could see a new shade of brown forming inside of Randall's petulant eyes. The new shade of brown reminded the lonely kid of wet dirt.

VI.

Kayla finished her conversation with Iris and set her phone down on the passenger seat.

A calm serenity now entered the hull of her Honda. The last five minutes of talking about boys drained her. Iris loved to talk boys. However, Kayla still couldn't remember the cashier's name from earlier in the night.

She thought about it for a couple minutes.

Alas, the only name coming back to her was her ex. And to be honest, regarding the cute boy from tonight, Kayla wasn't too sure if she was ready to date again. Recently, she found contentment in her solitary ways.

At heart, Kayla knew she would always be an introvert, welcoming the sight of her laptop, her favorite show, and the familiarity of her pink and purple fleece blanket.

She was almost home.

Kayla pulled up to the intersection of a four-way stop, thinking of the cashier again. She couldn't help but feel charmed by his words. Honestly, she couldn't remember a thing he said, but that wasn't important. To her, it was the *way* he said things. The cadence coming from each word; the soft, baritone notes that made her interior vibrate. It was a feeling she hadn't felt in a long time. Not with a boy at least. And as she sat there, pondering a Midwestern life with this gas station clerk, blue lights—*two dragon eyes in the middle of the night*—casted their brilliance over her. The ferocity of the beams burned her eyes, causing her to lift a hand in defense. Through her fingers, she made out the car on the other side of the intersection; the SUV from before; the car that wasn't the cops.

"What the fuck," Kayla whispered, squinting for more clarity.

Outside, across the intersection, a dark figure opened the driver's side door and appeared. With syncopated feet striking the road, the figure stalked around the door and closed it forcefully.

Thunk!

Kayla watched as the shadowy figure's legs wandered to the front of the SUV's hood, standing between the halogens in a blue glow.

Kayla watched with fear as the figure reached inside of itself. And squinting harder than ever, she realized that the figure was taking something out. She studied closer.

And suddenly, Kayla's eyes widened.

The dark figure held a pistol.

With a shot of adrenaline pumping into her heart, Kayla put the car into drive, steered left, and floored it. Tires squealing, smoke rising into the night sky, her Honda zoomed past the dark figure. And looking into the rearview mirror, heading in a new direction from home, she could sense the figure staring back at her.

"What the fuck are you?" Kayla shouted, looking at the diminishing shadow man.

Kayla picked up her phone to call the cops.

However, this part of town was a dead zone.

She saw no bars of connection on her phone's LED display.

And speeding down this wrong turn that led to another city, she held her phone out—waiting for a signal.

* * *

Smoke lingered in the lonely man's nostrils as he watched the girl's Honda scurry away. He studied the road she took and knew there wasn't much life between here and the next city. There would be no interference. And as he ruminated other dark contemplations, something inside of him told him to go home. However, another voice— much stronger—compelled him on.

The voice seemed very familiar to the lonely man.

What's the next move, kid?

He thought of marbles.

Shaking his head, the lonely man walked back to his SUV, feeling the weight of the Colt .45 in his hand. And as he entered the car, he placed the pistol in the passenger seat and regarded his reflection in the rearview mirror.

And in the mirror, seated behind him in the backseat, the lonely man saw the phantom figure of a fat, ginger boy.

Dark ooze spilled from the boy's gray and stitched skin. And his voice echoed in the lonely man's ears with a demonic vibrato.

Well?

The lonely man looked back to himself, smoothing out his remaining hair.

When's the wedding?

The lonely man brandished an uncomfortable smile.

"Shut up, Randall."

* * *

Nearby, a family of raccoons watched on as the license plate of a speeding SUV zoomed past them. To the creatures, the letters on the plate looked hieroglyphic; although, to the lonely man, fighting against the stream of time, they meant everything:

GRGA4VR

VII.

The lonely kid carved the message carefully into a white oak tree, finishing the last letter with a broken piece of glass. He wiped the sweat off his brow and stood back. Next to him, Georgia raised a hand to her cheek.

The lonely kid dropped the shard of glass and looked to Georgia—his eyes lost in the red cyclones rotating around her cheeks. He loved it when she blushed.

"Well," he said, "what do you think?"

Georgia moved her hand from her face and put it to his; her soft palm nestled against his cheek. A jolt of blood rushed underway; however, he composed himself.

"I love it," she said.

"I love you."

"Forever?" she asked.

"Forever."

They kissed each other. And for a while. The lonely kid's lips began to hurt, but he knew that the cause of the pain was nothing to halt. In fact, he would have kissed her until his lips turned to bone.

And opening his eyes mid-kiss, looking at Georgia's closed and intent eyes, the lonely kid had such a strange thought.

He thought about his own parents who must have had a similar experience like this years ago.

A powerful exchange of lips.

Although, the lonely kid thought about their current condition of love. Their love that only met when his father came home with his annual bonus, and when mother cooked his favorite meal. And watching them, from a distance, he never saw them kiss anymore. For when they did, it always felt so foreign.

How alien.

The lonely kid was used to the lack of affection from his parents, but now—kissing the love of his life—he wondered when he would lose this feeling. He wondered when the only thing to illuminate his heart would become a hot plate of seared beef tips and roasted potatoes.

He wondered when she would stop loving him.

The lonely kid stopped kissing her.

"What?" Georgia asked.

He took a couple of steps back and rubbed his lips.

"They burn," he said.

"I know," she said, walking towards him, "but I like it."

Georgia reached out for his face, but he grabbed her wrists. She pulled them back—almost wounded.

"What's wrong?" she asked.

"Nothing," he said, grabbing his head like a crystal ball, "I'm just an idiot lost in my mind."

Georgia watched him pace back and forth. The broken piece of glass lay nearby.

"What are you lost about?" she asked.

"I don't know," he said.

"Yes, you do."

"No, I don't."

"Yes, you do," she said, crossing her arms like a general.

The lonely kid sighed and walked to the white oak where he carved the message. He examined his markings.

Georgia followed him to the tree—albeit reluctantly.

And looking at the message, with tears in his eyes, the lonely kid reached out for her hand.

"Why?" she asked.

"Please."

"No, you stopped kissing me. Why should I hold your hand?"

"Because I need to know!" he yelled.

Georgia stepped back, shocked by his explosion. Her mouth hung open as the lonely kid wept. He sank to his knees by the tree and palmed his eyes. He hoped his hands would stop the tears; although, he knew this wave had to pass. These emotions had slept for far too long.

"I need to know," he began, "that you won't love me now...just to hate me later."

Georgia dropped to him.

"I don't want to end up like my parents," he continued, "I want to come home to a place of love."

Georgia began to cry. "I want that, too."

"I need to know," he said, "that these kisses we share will last until we're old."

Georgia nodded.

"Old enough," he said, "that we'll even wipe each other's asses."

Georgia chuckled through her tears.

"I'm serious, Georgia. I don't want to lose this feeling. I want it to last. I want us to grow," he said, pointing to the message in the tree's bark, "forever."

Georgia held him close, burrowing her face into his shoulder. He could feel her tears soaking through his shirt.

"I know," she said.

The lonely kid wiped away his eyes and helped her to her feet. Dusting the mud from his knees, he took a step back and looked at her in full. And as they stood apart, the message in the tree—**GRGA4VR**—dividing them, he smiled.

"I love you, Georgia."

Georgia wiped her eyes and walked towards him— wrapping her arms around his frame as she closed the distance.

"Forever," she said.

The lonely kid sighed in her embrace, sinking his face into the valley of her shoulder.

"Forever," he said.

He clutched her waist.

And shortly after, they began to sway.

As they danced to the sounds of the earth, kissing from time to time, a light sprinkling of rain began to fall from the sky. And against the day's sunshine, the soft rain was a sight the lonely kid would never forget.

In the summer rain, he held her closer.

And on her tip-toes, Georgia kissed the lonely kid's face. He followed her wet lips around his shimmering face for hours.

* * *

Two weeks later, on a regular day, Georgia was hit by a drunk driver on her way home from school. The hit killed her instantly. And at the funeral, standing between his parents who had fought the whole way there, the lonely kid held onto a rose.

"Forever," he whispered.

And as her closed casket entered the earth forever, the lonely kid clutched the rose's stem tighter—feeling the jagged thorns enter his palm.

"Forever," he strained.

And when it came time to drop his rose, standing by the cliffs overlooking her casket, he noticed blood spilling from his hand.

Overhead, as the lonely kid dropped the bloody rose onto Georgia's tomb, soft notes of thunder began to form.

VIII.

Kayla could hear the thunder overhead as she sped down the rural road heading elsewhere.

Her speedometer reached 85, but her sense of velocitation told her it wasn't fast enough.

She checked her mirrors for the SUV.

Although, nothing appeared in the proceeding darkness.

No blue headlights.

Kayla composed herself, dropping her acceleration.

She let out a big breath and checked her phone for signal.

Damn.

The empty road ahead paralleled the condition of her technological connection. Kayla placed her phone in her lap and kept her focus on the road. And as the mile markers passed by, she kept going over the dark figure who stood with a gun in his hand. She could discern the figure was male, but she wondered his purpose.

A serial killer?

Kayla's Honda decelerated to 70.

A friend of my dad's? No, who the fuck does that?

Kayla's Honda decelerated to 65.

The blue headlights lights appeared in Kayla's rearview. Their circular presence grew as the SUV closed the distance. Her Honda accelerated to 95—looking towards 100.

Who the fuck are you?

* * *

The lonely man clenched his steering wheel as his SUV zipped past the dark grasslands. Like a shark, thinking of *Jaws*, he could feel the distance closing in on the Honda. He could imagine a white, protective sheen glazing over his eyes; pale orbs reflecting the red taillights of a stranger's car.

The lonely man whistled an old tune as he connected his front bumper with the backside of her car.

Crack!

The Honda freed itself from its metal predator, revealing a crumpled trunk and the jagged remains of red glass.

The lonely man watched the glass fall to the consuming road and couldn't help but think of the time his uncle Kevin took him hunting in the snowy woods of Wyoming many years ago. He remembered his uncle sitting down on a decayed tree stump, wiping the frost off his massive eyebrows, and telling him the rules of hunting. And as a young boy, a rifle in his cold hands, he stood by his uncle and listened intently. However, back to the current situation, ramming the girl's car one more time—*crack!*—he forgot his uncle's most important rule from that day: *never chase the thrill, kid.*

* * *

Kayla screamed at the impact of the SUV. She had no time to process any of this. She could only rely on her flight. She kept her lead foot on the gas, increasing her speed, which by now maxed the Honda's limit. And trying to breathe, she looked in the rearview. However, the blue lights mystified any visual context; they burned too bright.

Kayla kept her focus ahead.

Somewhere.

And Kayla thought of her father.

Dad.

And Kayla thought of her dog.

Chubbers.

She thought of home.

Kayla envisioned herself on her father's recliner. It was a place she found solace in syndicated reruns and her father's phantom presence while he worked late.

Kayla could see the recliner perfectly.

And as she returned her thoughts back to the road—finding her breath—she saw the deer.

The Honda's windshield exploded on impact with the deer.

The deer itself flew to the right. Kayla tried to maintain control, steering wildly with glass in her face, but the blow itself caused her neurons to enter shut down mode. Kayla could see the creeping vignette around her eyes. And the last thing she could make out before the car veered off the road completely was the sign to her left which read Mile 81.

Kayla tried to articulate something as darkness plucked her fingers off the steering wheel.

The Honda dropped into a nearby ditch, catapulting itself in the air due to the speed. A collection of metal and glass glinted in the night sky as the vehicle realigned itself with the concept of gravity and plummeted back to earth.

And before impact, Kayla was already in the darkness.

She began to dream.

* * *

The lonely man stomped on his brakes as he watched the tortured Honda roll four times before it came to a complete stop. Chest rising, eyes refocusing, beads of sweat sprinted down the lonely man's face. He looked at the smoke beginning to plume over the remains of the Honda. And after an uncomfortable silence, he finally stepped out of his SUV. His pistol remained in the passenger seat.

The lonely man walked along the vehicular debris cautiously.

As he walked, natural sounds began to appear from the peripheral darkness: there were crickets, there were winds, and—creeping closer—there were the soft sounds of shallow, agonal breathing.

The breathing took the lonely man back to his hunting trip with his uncle Kevin when he was a kid. And during their objective sojourn for deer in the woods of Wyoming, they had bagged a doe. His uncle was proficient with his Remington rifle. And walking towards the doe who was tagged in the shoulder, weaving through snow-caked trees, Kevin told him to listen to the animal's sounds.

Do you hear that, kid?

He could.

It's never easy taking a life. Let's go and show God's creature some mercy. Sound good, kid?

He nodded.

And as the lonely man reached where the Honda had come to a stop, overlooking the small bluff of the ditch, he placed one of his hands to his mouth.

Do you hear that, kid?

Struck by his uncle's phantom words, the lonely man looked into the Honda and was struck by a sight far more powerful. Eyes focusing, he saw the girl in red's eyes looking back at him. Her wide eyes were familiar. Her eyes were jade spotlights from a past, yet only this time, there was no illumination. Any glimmer of light in them had extinguished.

The lonely man spilled a tear.

And as the smoke from the Honda creeped higher, he looked to his right and finally to his left.

There was no one else in sight.

The lonely man descended the slope of the ditch. And as he reached the base, he walked up to the car and crouched down.

He looked inside and trembled.

The lonely man wept quietly.

"Please don't leave me," he said.

* * *

In her final dream, Kayla could see the purple and orange sunset of Los Angeles clearly. And even more clearly, standing next to her, she could see the cashier from the convenience store she had met earlier tonight. She could picture his cute smile radiating along with the colorful sky. The image was perfect to her.

She began to speak softly.

And with her last breaths, Kayla could see the exotic sunset lower beyond the horizon of her existence. She could see the cashier from tonight's visage—much like his name—transform into obscurity. She could see the credits of her life fade into the infinite darkness. And with one last attempt, she tried to find the light.

She focused hard on the thought of the cashier's face, searching for the anchor of his name. However, it was too far gone.

Kayla took one final breath of air, and died saying random boy names.

* * *

The lonely man crouched next to the dead girl, crying softly until the landscape fell silent. Finally, he stood up and walked away.

"Goodbye, Georgia," he said.

And as the lonely man began his climb out of the ditch, his hands dirty, something in his periphery caught his attention.

He stared at the small object for a few seconds, listening to the natural sounds around him grow, before making up his mind.

Listening to the crickets beyond, with the far away sounds of settling thunder, the lonely man toyed with a keychain on his way back to his SUV.

Inside his car, with the doors closed and locked, the lonely man studied the blue beetle in artificial light. He gently brushed his thumbs over the grooves of its outline.

The lonely man sat there for some time before he put his SUV in reverse, made a point of turn, shifted into drive, and headed back the other way—leaving the destroyed Honda in his rearview.

And on his way home, the lonely man rubbed the blue beetle gently, whispering to himself a message he inscribed in tree bark many years ago.

IX.

Shutting off the switchboard for the store's lights, Ben thought of Kayla in the darkness.

He walked towards the front door to lock up, wondering if he would be able to find her on Facebook.

Ben figured a lot of girls in this city probably didn't have that name. He had never met a Kayla before. From his years in public education, most girls Ben knew had names like Becky or Sarah. And actually, funny enough, he once met a Beksarah. Such a strange name, Ben thought as he locked the store's front doors. And as he turned away to head out the back, the soft, growing sounds of sirens turned his attention forward.

Looking beyond the store's lonely gas pumps in the distance, Ben kept his focus on the building sirens. And after a growing crescendo of authority, he finally saw the fire trucks, the ambulances, and even the police fly by in a vibrant parade of red and blue.

The sight made Ben think of the fourth of July. He thought of those hot summer nights as a kid, awestruck and dumbfounded by the pretty lights in the sky. And oddly enough, Ben saw the passing display as somewhat comforting. However, he did feel bad for the receiving end of that parade. He imagined something really nasty must have happened for that sort of attention.

Walking towards the back doors, Ben took out his phone and opened his social media.

He contemplated the spelling of Kayla as he locked the back door.

The next morning, Ben walked up to the convenience store and noticed a parked car with a tall man sitting on its hood. The car looked officially vague—much like the man himself. Ben could see the gray in his sideburns. He also noted the gray suit and black shoes. *Very professional*, Ben thought. The tall man wore hair gel. The slick back look reminded Ben of someone younger. And strangely, he wondered if the man was self-conscious about his age— given the hairstyle.

Ben wondered how long the man had waited.

The tall man noticed Ben and adjusted his posture, sharpening up around the shoulders.

"Morning," Ben said.

"Morning, young man. Do you work here?"

"I do," Ben said, jingling a set of work keys. "It'll just be a couple of minutes until I get everything booted for the day."

"Booted?" the tall man asked.

"Right, I'm sorry," Ben said, "it's a computer term. I really mean it's going to take me a couple of minutes to turn on everything before I can check you out or give you some gas."

"Oh, no need, young man."

Ben focused on the words *young man*. The phrase helped him rule out if this guy was a hitman or a cop. His bet landed on the latter.

The tall man rose from his car, sending a slight shiver through Ben's spine, and brandished a gold badge.

Ben relaxed; he was thankful it wasn't the former.

"I just have a couple of questions for you," the man resumed. "My name is Detective Bodock."

Ben stared at the detective cautiously.

"And what can I help you with, Detective Bodock?" Ben asked, pointing to the front doors. "Do you mind if we chat inside actually?"

"Not at all," Bodock smiled. "By all means, you can get everything…*booted*. Is that what you said?"

"It was," Ben said, walking around the store. "Just need to enter from the back and I'll come around and open up the front. Give me a couple minutes, Detective."

"Of course."

Ben proceeded to the back of the store, unlocked the back door, thought of all his past sins, and entered. On his way to the front, he wondered if his internet search of *The Anarchist Cookbook* was catching up to him. It wasn't a serious search, Ben mused, unlocking the front doors. The search was just research for one of his short stories.

Ben opened the front door and welcomed the detective inside.

"Come on in," he said.

"Much obliged," Bodock smiled.

Both of them walked inside the dimly-lit store.

Ben kept his eyes forward to the register, while the detective next to him shifted his eyes from aisle to aisle.

Ben felt sweat under his armpits.

"Have a lot of customers come in here last night?" Bodock asked.

"Not too many, which, for a Friday night is strange."

"How so?" Bodock asked, leafing his fingers through a selection of chips.

"Well," Ben said, tidying up his register, "normally, for a Friday night, we get a lot of the Old Town crowd. If, you get what I mean."

"Night-lifers," Bodock smiled. "Is that right?"

"Right, detective. Those looking for a quick sense of sobriety often come through here. And to be honest, it's a great night for Doritos."

Bodock laughed, placing a bag of pork rinds back on the shelf.

"You're pretty funny. I imagine with that sense of humor you have many interesting conversations here."

Ben flipped the switch on a nearby circuit breaker, illuminating the store in a fresh sheen of fluorescence. In the harsh lighting, the detective appeared a lot older to Ben than before. He regarded the detective's youthful hairstyle again and smiled.

"Well, detective," he said, gesturing to the empty store like a prized gladiator, "I do my best to keep my sanity."

"Very good, young man," Bodock said, walking up to the counter. "And actually, I never got your name."

"It's Ben…Ben Marlowe."

"Marlowe," Bodock ruminated. "Huh, sounds real fancy, Ben."

"Thanks," Ben said. "I like to think it'll have a nice ring in my readers' mouths when they read my books one day."

"Oh, you're a writer?" Bodock asked.

"I dabble."

"And what do you like to write?"

"I don't know how to really describe it," Ben began, "I guess you could say I like to write fiction that's grounded. You know, *real*. And the interesting thing I like to do is put supernatural elements—like monsters—in the realism. Make it seem real, but foreign—*almost alien*—at the same time. To me, it's quite the juxtaposition."

Bodock laughed, relaxing his shoulders, and placing his hands on the counter.

"Well, I don't need to interrogate you to see you're an English major," Bodock laughed. "Now, that last word you used...juxta wha?"

"*Juxtaposition.*"

"Yeah, that one," Bodock nodded. "Now, what does that mean?"

Ben smiled, unsure of how to define it exactly. He had the general idea of the word. However, much like a lot of the higher-level words he spouted off from time to time, he usually winged their incorporation into his daily dialogues. Nobody, Ben thought, ever really challenged them.

"It just means side-by-side," Ben said.

"Side-by-side," Bodock registered. "You mean, just like me and this kiosk of keychains?"

Ben looked at the rotating kiosk, remembering Kayla and the blue beetle.

He smiled. "Sure, detective. Something like that."

Bodock nodded. "Good to know, Ben."

And shortly after, the detective sighed.

Ben watched as Bodock's face became less genial; a familiar chill began to creep up his spine as the detective talked in a new, professional tone.

"Thanks for the lesson," Bodock said. "But, to be honest, your writing sense seems a little bit unnecessary."

Ben felt somewhat attacked by what Bodock said. "And why's that, detective?"

Bodock reached in his suit jacket and pulled out a photograph.

"Because, Ben," Bodock said, "life itself is already filled with *monsters*."

Bodock showed Ben the photograph.

"Did you see this girl last night, Ben?"

Ben stared into the paper irises of the girl he sent a Facebook friend request to last night. He could tell that the photo he was looking at was a younger version of her. Possibly a college ID picture, he thought.

As Ben stared at Kayla's picture, remembering the sirens from last night, Ben felt his left leg shaking.

"Ben?" Bodock asked.

"Kayla."

Bodock withdrew the photo from Ben's gaze, checking it himself. "That's right, Ben. Did you know her?"

Ben felt the shaking in his left leg infect his right leg. He imagined his legs were made out of wood, splintering at the base.

"No," Ben said.

"No?" Bodock asked. "But her name?"

"I only met her last night, detective."

Bodock nodded. "Oh. I see, Ben."

"We talked for a good while."

"I see."

"Do you?" Ben asked, looking beyond the photograph into a romanticized future that could never be.

Bodock nodded. "I take it you both had a special conversation last night."

"Is she really dead?" Ben asked.

Bodock fixed his eyes on Ben.

After a brief moment, the detective lowered his gaze and nodded slowly.

"She was killed in a collision last night," Bodock began, "shortly after leaving here. From the wreckage we pulled out a receipt."

Ben nodded; his eyes remained glued on Kayla.

"It's funny though," Bodock said, "she didn't look like the smoking type."

"She was buying them for someone else...I think."

"Well, you guys really did have quite the conversation," Bodock said, putting the photograph away. "Now, Ben. I'm sorry if this is troubling for you. And I'm sure it is. But...I really need you to tell me something."

"What?" Ben asked, keeping his eyes where Kayla's photo used to be. "What else can I tell you?"

"Well," Bodock began, reaching his hand into another suit pocket. "We found *this* in the wreckage, too."

Bodock placed a small, Ziploc bag on the counter with a crumpled sheet of paper inside. At first, Ben thought it was a joint. However, on closer inspection, he knew what it was.

It was the receipt Ben gave Kayla last night before she drove to her end; the receipt that afforded Ben one more look.

Bodock smoothed out the receipt in the bag for a better optic. And as the detective did this, a strand of his hair—held before in a military phalanx of gel—popped out of place and fell against his furrowed forehead.

"There we go," Bodock finished.

Ben looked at the receipt and verified it. He could tell by the pink line on the right side of the paper that it was the one he gave Kayla. Ben remembered what the pink line on the receipt meant. He could hear his manager's echoes.

When the pink line shows up, that's when you know you're at your end. Time for a new roll, kid.

Bodock adjusted his hair and focused on Ben. "I need to verify if Kayla really bought this last night."

Bodock pointed at the receipt, his finger punctuating the pink margin.

Time for a new roll, kid.

"Did she buy the blue beetle, Ben?" Bodock asked.

Ben took his eyes away from the counter. They drifted somewhere beyond Bodock.

"Yes…but why?" Ben asked.

"Well," Bodock began, "that's because we couldn't find the keychain anywhere near the scene. I've had my lead investigators searching the surrounding area for hours, but, alas…nothing. They're just finishing up a secondary scan this morning, and I just wanted to make this certain."

Ben's eyes refocused on Bodock. "She bought it."

"That's what I figured, Ben."

Bodock sighed, placing the receipt back into his jacket, and looking to the floor. Ben could sense the detective was processing something.

A figurative jigsaw with legs, Ben thought.

Bodock finally perked up, stroking a beard that wasn't there, and feigned a small smile.

"Thank you, Ben," Bodock said, "I appreciate your help this morning.

Ben nodded.

Bodock reciprocated.

The two stood in silence for a couple of seconds.

Ben could feel Bodock trying to find the right words to say before departing; he always loathed the notion of forced sympathy.

He wished Bodock would just leave.

And much like the pink-colored receipt, Ben thought, it was time for a new roll.

Ben began tidying up his register.

Bodock nodded and tapped the register twice. "Just wanted to say I'm sorry, Ben. I understand. Just know it gets better with time. And trust me, I know that sounds pretty fucking cliché."

Ben nodded.

"And as someone who writes," Bodock continued, "I don't think I have to tell you that. Have a good day, young man."

Bodock began to walk out of the store. However, before his right hand touched the front door's handle, Ben asked him a question.

"What does all this mean, detective?"

Bodock stopped, looked to the video camera in the corner of the store, and told him.

Ben listened to Bodock's story—envisioning the size 13 shoe prints around the crime scene.

X.

The lonely teen watched the static overlap itself on the small television in his room. Monochromatic whispers— ominous callings of dread from beyond—spoke to him.

It had been five years since Georgia's death. And for the lonely teen, mentally, it had been much longer. The self-prescribed isolation to his room only added to the melancholy he felt day-in-and-day-out.

Nothing mattered to the lonely teen anymore: school, dreams, and even family became obsolete designs.

His mother cried every night for him.

And his father looked further into the bottle.

It had been a while since he spoke; however, the static kept its whispers, speaking to him through soft tones of dead air.

And he listened daily, waiting for Georgia's voice to break through.

Just to hear her voice one more time, he thought.

To hear his name spoken from those beautiful pink lips—*now gray and cracked with maggots seeping out!*

The whispers inside the lonely teen's head troubled him more than the ones in the television. The voices inside him had teeth; they ate through his skull; they exposed his brain to shotgun blasts of decay; they corrupted his memories; they warped his neurons; and they cemented the synaptic space associated with the girl he loved in darkness.

The lonely teen kept his darkened eyes on the static of the television and waited.

He kept his ears open.

And finally, he heard a voice…

>>

"Breaking news," a voice from the television said. "Last night, near Mile 81, heading towards El Dorado, a young woman was killed in a car crash. The accident landed her vehicle in a ditch. Police believe the young woman lost control after hitting a deer. The name of the victim has yet to be identified."

The lonely man sat close to his flat-screen; his dark eyes locked on the news anchor. As the news report on the television continued, the screen split—introducing a field reporter. In the second screen that appeared alongside the news anchor, a middle-aged field reporter—wearing a yellow suit jacket—stood near the familiar scene.

The lonely man remembered the road, the debris, and the breathing.

"Well," the news anchor said, "has there been any other developments on the scene?"

"Some," the field reporter said, holding his earpiece, "the authorities haven't released anything official. However, we've seen some officers scanning the area for something."

"Tampering?" the news anchor asked. "What do you think those officers are searching for?"

"Not too sure," the field reporter said, directing the camera to the scene of the crash, "but as you can see, they don't seem satisfied yet."

The camera shot on the field reporter's screen zoomed into the scene, refocusing for a second to show a pair of officers canvassing the area.

"We'll just have to wait on that police statement," the news anchor said.

And as the news anchor thanked the field reporter's coverage, the sounds of the lonely man's television slowly transformed into a familiar static. The sound of the digital screaming brought him an odd comfort than the reality of his news. And sitting in his recliner—rubbing the blue beetle keychain and listening for a familiar voice—the lonely man sat there for a long time.

The next morning, the lonely man took a cold shower. Afterwards, he made himself breakfast: a package of bacon, six eggs, eight pieces of toast, and a pitcher of orange juice.

A meal for a family, consumed by one.

And wiping his mouth with his forearm, the lonely man picked up his car keys, his wallet, and his nametag.

He had work this afternoon.

He put on his size 13 shoes.

On his way out of his apartment, the lonely man caught his reflection and stood there looking at himself.

He regarded his age. The years since.

And after a few moments of quiet contemplation, he began to sob loudly. The sobs turned into quiet whimpers as he walked outside and across the parking lot to his SUV.

Inside his car, looking for eye drops in the glove compartment, the lonely man kept his eyes on the pistol from the night before. Its barrel—which pointed at him—reminded him of a tunnel he drove through last winter: a cold, dark shortcut heading elsewhere.

XI.

The father arrived at home a little before nine. He spent the last few days working late to keep his mind busy. Since Kayla's funeral, and the bereavement, he grew tired of his house. He grew tired of watching reruns while the empty room on the second floor festered a sense of desolation that spread throughout the rest like a virus.

Stepping down from his truck, holding his bag of tools from a long day of construction, the father noticed a pair of blue headlights off in the distance approaching.

And walking towards his porch, the blue headlights grew brighter as the SUV drove by, spotlighting the father's house like a lonely lighthouse nestled on the edge of a bluff.

A precipice, the father considered, in these recent days of darkness.

Living without his wife, and now his daughter, the father's motivation to do anything nowadays felt slim around his waist, and not just because of his lack of appetite.

The father found himself most nights weighing the pros and cons of suicide.

He often thought of his brother in the next city over; however, they hadn't talked in years until the funeral. He realized that the act would have no familial weight. In all honesty, the only thing keeping him alive was the eight-year-old pug laying on the kitchen floor as he walked inside his house.

"Chubbers," the father said.

Kayla's dog.

He tapped the older pug on his way to the refrigerator with his shoe.

"You hold down the fort?"

Chubbers let out a grunt; his chubby cheeks flapped against the floor.

Inside the refrigerator, the father searched for food. Since everything, the produce turned to *Bud Light*, the grain turned to *Blue Moon*, the meat turned to *Johnny Walker*, and the sugar turned to *Coke*. He considered the options.

"What do you think, Chubs?" the father asked. "Should I have a salad or a steak?"

Chubbers grunted.

"Steak it is."

The father grabbed the JW and Coke and headed for the sink. The stockpile of dirty dishes was another reminder of his loneliness. From the sink, he looked for the cup that seemed the cleanest.

Scraping some gunk off from the inside of a mug, he poured his meal inside and headed for the living room.

"Come on, Chubs."

Slowly, the pug lifted itself up and followed the father.

A couple minutes passed as the father sat watching his favorite shows.

A couple more minutes passed before Chubbers finally fell asleep in his lap. And watching the pug snore sweetly, he thought of Kayla. He remembered how small and warm Kayla felt as a baby; he remembered her sweet spasms forming into small smiles. They were early images he held onto for comfort. They were images in a sequence ended too early, but never forgotten.

The father cried softly, rubbed Chubbers' head, and removed a bottle of pills from his jacket.

And looking at the pills, he remembered what the dealer told him last night.

Make your favorite drink, take these, and you'll sleep forever, my man.

"Forever," the father whispered.

To him, it was a word that seemed to contradict existence; a word that became a human paradox; a word that felt like a futile thing said to others to acquiesce feelings of insecurity.

A fucking empty promise.

The father opened the pill bottle carefully, grabbed his liquid meal, and closed his eyes.

"Forever," he said, thinking of Kayla.

And right before the father poured the pills into his mouth, he felt the darkness behind his shut eyelids transform to blue.

Opening his eyes, the father saw a bright, blue light shining from outside into his living room window.

The father wondered if it was his brother coming to retrieve his wife's casserole dish. A parting "gift" from the funeral.

Placing the pills and his drink on a nearby table, the father removed Chubbers from his lap and got up.

He walked to the window, shielded his eyes for clarity, and noted that it wasn't his brother. The blue halogen lights belonged to a much nicer vehicle. It was the SUV from before. The one he spotted before entering his house.

And nearby, Chubbers began to stir. The pug could sense something in the air. The dog's murmurings were lined with fear.

The father wondered if it was that detective with more leads on the case. He couldn't remember his name. The only thing he could remember was the hair gel.

Boondock?

The father shook his head, heading for the front door.

Regardless of what the detective and his team were trying to prove, the father didn't believe there was foul play involving Kayla's death. All evidence pointed to shitty circumstances, and he himself knew his fair share. The notion of a missing keychain wasn't enough to keep hope alive. The father didn't like to entertain wild detective theories. In fact, the whole thing felt like another step away from closure.

The father opened his front door, remembering what the deer looked like on the side of the road. The deer that took his girl to heaven.

He stepped onto his porch.

"Hello?" the father asked, shielding his eyes from the SUV's blue spotlights. "Is that you, detective?"

A dark figure appeared from the vehicle.

The father squinted, making out a shape unfamiliar.

"It's late, mister. I don't know what you're up to, but whatever it is you're selling, or trying to get into, I'm not interested. Now, I'm only going to tell you this once: leave."

The dark figure began to approach the father.

"Listen," the father began, taking a step back, "I've been through a hell you couldn't imagine. Don't think I won't fu..."

The father's threat trailed off into the cold air like a lost echo searching for a landing. And as the dark figure walked up to him, revealing himself, the father noticed the Colt .45 pistol.

"Mister...?"

As the dark figure stood less than two feet away, the father could make out his details. He could see the man behind the bright, blue lights. The father saw the thinning hair, the pudgy cheeks of a bad diet, the wire-framed glasses of old age, and the dark eyes—surrounded by a sea of red—with tears spilling from them.

The man was completely nondescript to the father.

"Mister, what do you want?"

The lonely man raised his pistol to the father's head.

"Wait a minute," the father trembled. "What do you want? Who are you?"

The lonely man stared intently at the father. And shortly after, he turned the pistol around in his hand and invited the father to take it.

The father looked at the pistol incredulously.

"Take it," the lonely man uttered through tears. "Just take it."

"I—"

"Take it!" the lonely man shouted.

The father took the pistol automatically, unfamiliar with its weight.

The lonely man dropped to his knees in front of the father like a pastor genuflecting at an altar.

"I'm sorry," the lonely man said.

"For what?" the father asked.

The lonely man slowly reached into his pants; he gripped something tightly.

And with his other hand, the lonely man beckoned for the father's other hand. The one that didn't struggle with the pistol.

"Give me your hand," the lonely man said.

The father looked on with reticence but finally obliged.

And holding the father's hand, the lonely man removed his hand from his pants and connected it with the father's.

The father could feel the warmth of the small object the lonely man placed in his hand.

The lonely man slowly released the father, keeping his eyes to the ground. And as this dark figure stared at the darker dirt, the lonely man told the father who he was.

The lonely man began to confess.

"Forgive me, Georgia."

And as the father listened to the sobbing man, staring at the blue beetle keychain—hearing the faraway sounds of thunder encircle his mind—the weight of the loaded Colt .45 came back to him.

And shortly after the man he never met before was done speaking, a deafening silence followed.

A white silence that wept as the first real drop of rain—in years—landed between them from above.

XII.

The ashen sky over the town soon turned to blue. It had been a couple of years for Ben since everything had occurred with Kayla. Since then, he graduated, found a girlfriend, and became an English teacher.

The school wasn't Ben's alma mater, but he realized he looked better in maroon anyway.

And spending a Thursday afternoon with his girlfriend, they both walked to a local coffee shop for some drinks. Ben's girlfriend always loved to drink matcha, which reminded him of algae. And Ben liked to drink green tea. He had recently read something about its effects on metabolism.

And as they sat in the coffee shop, Ben and his girlfriend bonded over people watching. Ben's girlfriend was a behavioral therapist, so she always found body language—*para language*, as she always corrected him—fascinating. She could look at a person, deduce their zodiac, their anxieties, and their desires from the way they moved their arms, looked around, and even sneezed. Ben loved testing her, watching her eyes light up as he pointed to her next diagnostic. And watching her analyze, Ben remembered the first time he saw her in class, not knowing at the time what her lips felt like; not knowing how she would wake up in the middle of the night when her dreams turned dark; and not knowing at the time how she farted a little when she laughed. All these details so foreign on the onset were now a part of his living memory. Memories found in his stream of time.

They drank, they laughed, and soon realized they were running late for an engagement they agreed to. A game night, Ben remembered, realizing how he never enjoyed communion over small figures and laminated boards.

On their way out of the coffee shop, Ben patted his shorts, searching.

"What's up, babe?" his girlfriend asked.

"I think I left my keys on the table. I'll be right back."

"Okay," she said, pulling out her phone.

"I'll just stalk acquaintances," she continued.

Ben smiled and walked back inside the coffee shop. As he walked to their previous table, he noticed a beautiful girl sitting there holding his keys. She had a familiar look. Her green eyes evoked some distant memory within him as he watched her.

"Excuse me?" Ben asked.

"Are these yours?" the beautiful girl asked, jingling his keys playfully.

"Yes," he said, expecting a quick return.

The beautiful girl narrowed her eyes, sucking in air through small, soft-looking lips.

"How do I know these are yours?" she asked.

Ben smiled. "You're kidding, right?"

"Maybe," she said with a smile. "Don't I know you from somewhere?"

"I don't think so," Ben said.

"Are you sure?" she asked.

"Yeah," Ben said, looking to his keys. "Do you mind? I'm actually running late."

"I know I know you," she said firmly. "I'm sure I do."

Ben smiled, remembering an old feeling he felt somewhere in his faded memories. Somewhere in the opaque stream of his past.

Somewhere.

However, Ben took his keys, told the strange girl to have a good day, and walked outside to the sun-lit sidewalk.

>>

"What took you so long, babe? Who was that?"

"I don't know," Ben said, jingling his keys.

"Really?" she asked.

"I don't," Ben said, grabbing her hand, "and I don't care."

"Really?" she asked.

Ben smiled with his eyebrows.

Ben's girlfriend looked at him closely, studying him—searching.

He stared back at her—revealing.

And looking at him, she smiled.

"I love you, Ben," she said.

"I love you, too," he said.

They kissed.

And as they both walked northbound, heading to their game night, Ben's past stayed down south, elsewhere in time, stored between an empty freezer—an array of forgotten gas pumps—and Someone Great.

June Bug and Oscar Wilde

They talked about their plan on the way there.

The spot wasn't too much further now.

The truck carried along the road.

The plan was simple: June Bug would do the distracting and Frank would do the killing. It had been at least two years since the last time; therefore, Frank felt a little rusty. The weight of the pistol, nestled in a holster kissing his ribs, reminded him of his age.

It was bad enough that June Bug had hung all those mirrors in their home recently. Frank couldn't walk five feet without being reminded of his aging portrait. He thought of the writer Oscar Wilde in those moments but couldn't place why. Like many references from the past, dormant in the mind, they often blurred when given a chance to taste sunlight. However, looking into those portals of vanity, always smudged with fingertips, Frank noted the gray hair on his head; the sharp wrinkles that dug into his long, pale face; the sunken cheeks that made him look malnourished despite the meals.

Frank adjusted the pistol at his side, blinking the reality of the oncoming road back into his consciousness. Next to him, June Bug fidgeted with her curly hair.

"You think we'll get lucky like last time and get a couple?" June Bug asked.

"Maybe," Frank smiled.

"I hope so," she said, folding her knees up and resting her tennis shoes on the dash. "I hope they're big and fat."

"Well," Frank said, reaching for his smokes, "this is America."

June Bug laughed. Frank watched her chest rise and fall with each chuckle.

He was glad to see and hear it.

"You want one?" Frank asked, pulling out his cigarettes.

"Not yet," she said, "I'll have one after. Just like sex."

Frank placed the cigarette in his mouth, digging for his white lighter. He gave June Bug a side-eye she knew well. A clever look that bordered the lines of quizzical and romance.

"Well...call me greedy then," Frank said with the cigarette in his mouth, lighting it.

June Bug laughed, rolling her eyes to the window where she kept them on the stars that hung in the blue, moonlit sky above them.

As the road in the headlights passed underneath his truck, Frank looked to his left and regarded the dark countryside.

"Big and fat," June Bug mused to the moon, "big and fat."

"That's right," Frank said.

He kept his eyes on the rolling darkness, unsure of what he was looking at.

*   *   *

June Bug was a lot younger than Frank.

Whenever the two would go out to shop or grab a bite at a local restaurant, people in their town often regarded them as father and daughter. Although, one day, getting some lunch at a local bar and grill, June Bug decided to grab something else of Frank's under their table. And still stroking, their waitress came up for their check and could tell what was going on. Despite Frank's consistent stoicism—an expression he only let up for June Bug—he couldn't hide the elation. The waitress stormed away to get her manager. Frank finished and left two twenties on the table. He figured the extra Jackson would cover whatever mess he made on the carpet.

Shortly after the gross incident, the whole town knew about their situation. Eyes, from every age and angle, casted a shadow on the pair wherever they went. Older women wondered where June Bug's parents were, and most of the men wondered how an old SOB like Frank could pull a fine beauty. Frank's wealth was no secret, but his net worth couldn't have been more than your average farmer in these parts. The townsfolk sat around, eating their lunches, often speculating the pairing. However, despite the popular stigma, the two didn't care. And very seldom, spending afternoons doing whatever they pleased on acres of fantasy, Frank and June Bug seldom left their home. With all the land that Frank owned—inherited by his late and hardworking father—he let June Bug roam the property freely.

He often wondered if that was why she stayed with him for so long. He let June Bug do whatever she wanted with him and his land. Like an artist regarding a blank canvas, he allowed her to make a home for herself. And despite the mirrors that plagued every wall of his home, Frank rather enjoyed her presence and décor. Being an older man in the company of a younger woman revitalized his earlier self. As well, it galvanized his sex drive. The thought of a parallel life as a grandfather sometimes crept in his aging mind at night, but Frank always knew from childhood that he would die a bachelor. His parents' marriage—volatile and cold—also contributed to this decision. He couldn't bear the idea of holding all that emotional weight with a wife and kids. He reckoned they would take all of his time away from the things he really enjoyed doing. The things he did in the remote shed that sat near the creek that bordered his and another farmer's property line.

Things, Frank smiled, that June Bug also enjoyed.

*   *   *

As Frank stared into the darkness on their way to the spot—still smoking his cigarette—he couldn't help but notice his reflection in the truck's skewed side-view mirror. Each drag from the cigarette revealed the aforementioned details of his present—and old—appearance. As well, the orange glow of the cigarette added a sickly pall to his self-consciousness. He once again thought of Oscar Wilde. The word "picture" hung in his memory for a few seconds, but he shook his head. June Bug didn't seem to notice. Which was probably a good thing. Frank didn't want her to have any concern. Not tonight.

She kept her eyes on the stars.

Possibly somewhere beyond, Frank thought.

And watching her profile—youthful with many miles still ahead of her—Frank wondered how much longer she would stay with him if he let her.

Frank took one last look into the side-view mirror, baring a neglected smile, and shortly hid the foreign expression away.

It didn't take long for Frank to fix the mirror's rotation back to the road. And taking one last drag, he filled his lungs with smoke and threw the smoldering cigarette out the window.

The cigarette bounced off the road, scattering embers like a miniature firework.

"Are you okay, Frank?" June Bug asked.

"Yeah, why?"

"You didn't finish your cigarette."

"So?"

"You never waste one."

"Don't read into it, June. I promise this book's not as interesting as you think."

She smiled. "Yes, it is."

"Not for too much longer," he said.

"What's that supposed to mean, Frank?"

He adjusted his pistol which began to dig its barrel into his side. "Nothing. Forget it. We're almost there."

"Did I do something recently?" she asked.

Yes, he thought, you're still here...why haven't you left?

"No," he said, patting her thigh, "it's fine, June. Let's not spoil the fun for tonight."

She didn't believe him. He figured he should bring up something.

"Alright," Frank said, "you've put up a lot of mirrors recently at home. And…"

He searched for whatever he was trying to say. However, he couldn't help but think of Oscar Wilde once again. And even more ironic, Frank thought, is that he had no idea what the old writer even wrote. The word "picture" hung closer to him in the balance of his mind and he reached for it.

"And?" June Bug asked, her back against the passenger door.

"And…I've been having a hard time regarding my mug, June. My picture. I don't know why, but it makes me think of that old writer Oscar Wilde."

"Oscar Wilde?" she asked.

"Yeah…I don't know why. But I don't like it either."

June Bug crossed her arms and furrowed her brow. Frank couldn't help but imagine her at five-years-old doing the same thing. Despite some wrinkles, he thought, she still had a childish face that would follow her if she got to his age.

And maybe then, staring into an antique mirror of her own, she would understand him.

"I still don't understand, Frank. What are you trying to say to me? What does any of this have to do with Oscar Wilde?"

"Now June," he said, reaching for her, "it's not a big deal. Just something that's been on my mind."

June Bug didn't accept his hand and Frank let it dangle for a bit until it found its place back on the steering wheel.

"Look," he said, "it doesn't take a Sherlock to see that I'm an old fart. With all those mirrors at the house I can't help but look at how old I've gotten. Despite my vigor, the reflection shows me for what I am. To me and to you."

"And what are you to me?" June Bug asked, a sneer forming.

"Okay," Frank said, processing the road and his thoughts at the same time, "listen…I'm just rambling now. I didn't mean to put words in your mouth. Moral of the story is that I'm old. The mirrors just highlight that I guess. I've been a bit more conscious of the looks we get in town as well. Hell, I probably am older than your father."

"I don't know my father."

"Right. Like I said, it's just been a little foggy up there in my mind. I can't deny my age, and the mirrors would never let me anyways. That's all, June. I promise."

June Bug's sneer dissipated. In its place, a neutral set of lips wavered in the middle of a processing face. Frank could see her thinking. For some reason, he wondered if she even knew who Oscar Wilde was.

"Do you fear that I see you as that 'old fart,' Frank?"

Frank listened to the wind, unsure of what direction he was going now. And as he focused on the road—empty for many miles to each side—he reckoned this spot would do.

"Frank?" she asked. "Did you hear what I said?"

Pulling the truck onto the side of the lone highway, Frank shut off the engine and closed his eyes. June Bug watched as he sank into his chest with a deep breath.

"Frank?" she asked, reaching for his arm.

He brushed her away.

"Frank?" she asked.

Listening to the low hum of the truck's engine diminish—becoming one with the serenity of the breathing world—Frank took out his pistol from his holster and placed it on the seat between them. June Bug stared at it cautiously.

"Are we at the spot, Frank?" she said, looking around, "is this it?"

It wasn't.

"Yes, June Bug. We're here."

June Bug forced a smile; an expression to salvage some joy for the remaining night.

"It looks different from before, Frank. Are you sure? I remember more trees."

He was.

"I am, June Bug."

"Okay, Frank," she said, looking over her shoulder to the dark road behind them, "what's the next move? Should I lay on the road while you ambush them from behind? Should we play unsuspecting father and daughter?"

Sitting there, regarding her usage of the word play, Frank didn't know.

"Frank?"

He opened his eyes and looked to June Bug. As she waited for the right set of headlights—big and fat—he noticed her jugular undulating in the moonlight with all the right signs of composure.

June Bug was focused.

She was anticipatory.

And most of all, unlike him, she was young.

"We wait," Frank said, raising a hand of his own to his throat. Fingers pressed, eyes closed, he checked his own heart rate.

"And what are we waiting for?" she asked.

"I don't know," he said, struggling to find a count. "You should have a smoke."

Otra Vez

Crack!

Jusepe rose from his nightmare clutching his thundering chest. His wide eyes frantically scanned the entirety of his tent for recalibration.

Thinking of tamed horses—a tip he once heard from an elder—Jusepe closed his heavy eyes and breathed deeply. His tranquil thoughts calmed the proverbial stampede of hooves inside of him.

Chest settling, Jusepe continued breathing.

Inhale...

Exhale...

Inhale...

With the cold air of the Great Plains entering his tent, Jusepe couldn't help but remember the nightmare that rocked him awake.

Exhale...

He couldn't help but remember the figure.

Inhale...

The mythic man—wrapped in ripped clothing—whose decayed fingers and fossilized teeth grasped and gnashed at Jusepe's throat.

Exhale...

The creature who spoke to him before the eternal darkness.

"Otra vez," Jusepe said impulsively.

Alone, the utterance brought forth a haunting wind which flapped the walls of Jusepe's nomadic domicile. The harsh gust worried him. The last thing he needed right now was his shelter to collapse.

Jusepe got to his feet, exited his tent, and checked the tent's support systems. The strings that held the suspension were solid, and so were the metal rods that dug deep into the soil. He inspected the tent's walls, questioning the durability of the buffalo skin. And stroking a careful finger against the wall—the stretched dermis—it held fine.

Just like the animal itself, it was strong.

The thought brought forth a small chuckle and recollection from Jusepe. He thought of the battle with the buffalo which now provided him shelter. How the beast charged him with the conviction of a devoted warrior. How he lucked out, dodging the creature's vengeful head, providing him with the perfect opportunity to strike its grand throat with his iron dagger.

Walking back inside, Jusepe remembered the buffalo's death cry clearly.

The agonizing, bestial cadence of death.

And for some reason, the recollection of sound brought his mind back to his recent dream.

Jusepe remembered the mythic man's ghostly claws digging into the soft flesh of his neck.

He winced, shaking the recollection away.

Inhale…

Back inside his tent, Jusepe could feel the proverbial horses inside him stirring, their restless hooves meandering.

Exhale…

Jusepe grabbed his fur jacket, another gift from the buffalo, and put it on.

The Great Plains were a cold place at night.

And looking for his dagger, Jusepe walked to his bed roll and searched his bag. He unwound the string that held the bag together. And as he did so, he couldn't help but feel a presence behind him.

The hair on the back of his neck stood as a gust of wind rolled around his shoulders like a ghostly necklace. In the wind, he was certain he heard the phrase again.

Otra vez

Wincing, almost dropping the string, Jusepe shook his head.

Inhale…

He knew better than to utter the phrase again, despite its mysterious allure.

Exhale…

Jusepe finished untying the bag and laid the loose cloth on the dirt next to his bed roll. He looked through the contents of his bag carefully, searching for the iron dagger.

However, looking again, it wasn't there.

For some strange reason, he felt that it was outside.

Otra vez

Hearing the piercing phrase in the distance—not far from his tent—he turned his attention to the exposed door and to the rolling land. The Great Plains invited him to exit his shelter. The land itself seemed to breathe at his feet.

Focusing on his breathing, taming the wild mares inside, Jusepe cautiously approached the door. The path ahead was cold for Jusepe with each step he took. And as he reached the door, he heard the familiar phrase getting closer like some misplaced echo coming home.

Jusepe peered his head out of his tent and looked both ways.

And regarding nothing but the moon's blue hue over the rolling scenery, Jusepe turned back to rest inside. Although, as his gaze returned to settle on his bed roll, he felt the wind tapping a spectral digit on his shoulder.

"Otra vez," the wind whispered into Jusepe's ear.

Inhale…

Jusepe's eyes and mouth opened wide, but despite everything his elder had taught him, the horses inside were set free.

His chest thundered inside of him and he couldn't breathe.

"Otra vez," the wind spoke.

But Jusepe couldn't reply.

"Jusepe?" the wind asked.

Hearing the billowing voice of dread, Jusepe could feel the decayed fingers of death digging deeper into the back of his neck.

"Jusepe?"

He could see the horses inside him as well.

"Otra vez."

With black fur and red eyes, the horses charged on within him. Jusepe reckoned they were running towards an exit. A crimson portal that would allow them to burst from his chest and ride into the rolling lands of the Great Plains forever.

Above, mixed with the charging hooves inside him,

Jusepe heard thunder.

Otra. Vez.

The fingers of the unknown entity—*the mythic man*—closed around Jusepe's neck.

Inhale…

And finally, moved by the manipulations of death, turning back to face the tent's door, Jusepe saw his dagger.

Otra Vez

The iron dagger was lodged in the figure who stood in front of him.

"Exhale, Jusepe," the figure whispered through bloody mouthfuls that fell to the earthly floor.

With insects weaving through its remaining frame, covered in sinewy muscle that turned the color of rotten pomegranates, it was a buffalo.

Jusepe's iron dagger stuck out from under its neck.

"Otra vez," the buffalo said, spilling blood all over Jusepe's bed roll.

Otra—

The fingers around Jusepe's neck squeezed, and the last thing he saw was lightning.

Crack!

Jusepe rose from his nightmare clutching his thundering chest. His wide eyes frantically scanned the entirety of his tent for recalibration.

And settling down, looking into the never-ending Great Plains through the tent's exposed door, Jusepe thought of horses.

Author's Note: this story is dedicated to my late grandmother, Helen Pacholski. Mrs. Blue Bird.

Steel Beams

My grandmother lived a great life.

It's hard for me to even piece it together for you to paint a picture, but if you could look into her eyes—mint-colored whirlpools of comfort—you'd see a timeless wonder throughout the ages; a set of eyes, like a television, that stayed true from sepia to technicolor.

I'll never forget my grandmother telling me about the buckets of beer she would bring to her elders who played cards outside of bygone storefronts. I'll never forget the story she told me of the man she loved before my grandfather.

And riding with my father, on our way to buy my dying grandmother a new dryer for her home, I'll never forget the way she looked at me last year, up late on her living room couch, and asked me the most important question of my life.

Are you happy?

Now who knows how to truly answer that question?

Are you happy?

Doesn't that question transcend age only to become a perennial curse for the living?

Are you happy?

I want to ask my father the question as he drives down some industrial road. However, I hold my tongue. The various neighborhoods of Chicago roll on by. I ask myself how could he be happy with his mother on the verge of the afterlife? For all I know, he must be an emotional wreck. I'm just grateful we can distract ourselves for a while by going for this new dryer. The old one busted not too long ago, and I looked online for nearby, secondhand appliance stores.

Luckily, one checked out.

Two weeks ago, my grandmother was put on hospice.

The medical technicians came into her home and installed the last bed she would ever sleep on. I arrived not too long after that with my father. The image of her old bed—a wonderfully massive queen with unique, ornamental designs—placed up against the wall in her back room was a troubling sight.

I remember it always being horizontal.

Not vertical.

And you know, it's funny how metaphorical the notion of being vertical really is. Most people use the term as a sign of good health Ask any old-timer who probably still listens to *Elvis* or *Sinatra* and they'll tell you the wonders of being "vertical." However, looking at her vertical, sagging mattress up against the wall, looking like a starved prisoner with a protruding belly, it was hard for me to stomach its new position.

It was just as tough seeing the new bed in my grandmother's room. All those new hydraulics; all those new pneumatic manipulations.

All those steel beams.

—

My father taps his finger to the tune of some song way before my time. Our rental car continues on in search of a new dryer.

The Yacht Rock radio announcer leads his listeners into the chorus of some song, and I often wish I was born earlier to know the words. My father sings along while I parrot after him, trying to build a stronger moment of connection. My relationship with my father isn't bad or anything. I just work for it more than usual nowadays.

Perhaps it's due to getting older.

I want him to know I care about him.

You know, before it's all over.

Before…

My father's done so much for me already. He's helped me through college, motivated my writing career, and even showed me how to change a tire at the age of 25. To be honest, I would still have to watch a video on YouTube to change it properly, but his willingness to model things never left me. He'd lay out the process—*all the nuts and bolts*—ask me questions, and I would nod—regardless of understanding a single thing.

It's quite a feeling to have that attention.

Even at 25.

I don't know how to describe it, but there's a timeless youth to a father's advice even beyond adolescence.

It's quite reassuring.

I often think about how much I'll miss the wisdom when I'm older and he's gone. Although, he's still here. And so am I.

I begin to mumble the question—*are you happy?*—but my father cuts me off.

"Are we going the right way?" he asks.

The radio itself fades into the subaudible of Chicago's industrial sounds as I pull out my phone to reassure my father and—quite honestly—myself. All these reveries, you know. Checking my phone, I often wonder if I've been daydreaming my entire life.

I go through my phone.

I show my father the screen.

"Vargas Appliances," he says, nodding.

That's the name of the store that checked out.

My phone's GPS continues to guide us there even though my father likes to think he "has it." I think it's fatherly intuition. Although, he did live here for a large portion of his life. Regardless, I know he's grateful for the technical support to make sure we get to Vargas safely.

There's too many dead-ends in Chicago, my father says. Too many reports of violence, a voice echoes. The last thing our family needs right now is another loss.

And I know for sure times have changed since my father last lived here. I see it on his brow as he cruises along a newer Chicago. I wonder if anything in his senses brings him back to the older Chicago he used to roam.

As we get closer to Vargas, my father takes a left turn and asks whether the place is going to be on the left or right.

I inform him the right. The rental car shifts into the right lane and we await the oncoming sign.

In red, rustic letters the sign displays the name "Vargas." The sign reminds me of another bygone era. Maybe not one of buckets of beer but possibly fresh ground beef from a local farm.

Arriving, my father puts the car in park and we both survey the store.

We see old washers and dryers nestled up against the storefront. They don't look so great to be honest. In fact, the whole scene looks almost apocalyptic. I daydream of venders selling out their wares from the hulls of each of these appliances. My father makes a sound of displeasure.

"Are you sure this is the place that checked out?" he asks, keeping his hand tight on the car's automatic shifter.

Are you happy?

The question creeps again. I see the uncertainty on his brow.

The heaviness.

I sense his impulse to downshift into D and drive the hell out of here.

I take one more look at the sign—*Vargas Appliances*—and check the browser on my phone. I know it's the right place, but if it eases my father's nerves, I'll do it.

To be honest, I'd hate to send my father and I into a situation straight out of some twisted film.

I could throw a punch, but I'm no Charles Bronson.

"This is the place, Dad. Here," I say, showing him the image of the storefront on my phone. "I know it's not the prettiest, but sometimes that's where you find the most treasure."

He smiles, taking his hand off the shifter. His brow opens up as well, releasing the corrugated ripples on his forehead.

"Are they even open?" he asks, craning his neck.

"Yeah," I say, seeing the shifting figure of a person behind the glass I can only imagine is Vargas.

"Alright," he says, "let's find some *treasure*."

We get out of the car, take in the fresh air of Southside Chicago, and walk up the graveyard of rusted appliances. As we approach the front door, a small man unlocks a sliding bolt and greets us with a smile. It's a welcome view, I think. Beyond him, silhouettes of washers and dryers reside in various rows. They seem to be in better condition. Nothing in comparison to the scattered remains that decay around the store. I look back to my father and he nods.

Are you happy?

Reluctantly—possible unsure—I nod back.

We enter Vargas Appliances and begin our search for the new dryer.

—

Are we happy?

I look around Vargas Appliances and ask myself that question. From a once over, I realize the online reviews were more graceful than realistic. Colossal wrecks line the walls on the inside. I'm reminded of Percy Shelley's poem "Ozymandias" as I think about how these rusted washers and dryers used to rule for their ancient families at a time. Once great machines, now second-hand scrap. My poetic daydream—one of too many—is interrupted by the man who must be Vargas.

He wears a flannel jacket, denim jeans, and a Chicago Bulls hat. His skin is the color of peanut butter. He speaks with no accent—which surprises me.

"We have more in the back?" Vargas says, watching my dad circle around a dryer.

"Is this gas?" my father asks, placing his hands on the top of the dryer.

"No, that's electric. We have some gas ones over there."

Vargas points and my father walks with a sharp automaticity.

I standby, checking out the rest of the store.

My mind is not as focused as my father. He was a military man. Still is in his countenance. Served his country and his family for over 20 years with an objective eye and a broad stride.

As I remember my father from early days, he's always been a pragmatic and focused man. He could walk into a store with a list and be out in under two minutes flat. I always appreciated that about him.

His intention.

Whenever I would go shopping with my mother, which always took twice as long—and in a lot of ways tested my patience—I would often think of my father's stride down various aisles and hallways. A similar one I see as he marches regarding Vargas' direction.

My dad isn't a hulking guy, but he's pretty formidable when you factor in his weight and build. Looking around in Vargas' shop, noting the grime on the floor, and the overall condition of the neighborhood, I'm grateful for his frame. Despite the feelings of vulnerability, it's reassuring to know my father could take Vargas if anything were to go awry. It's a passing thought—intrusive as they say—but nevertheless comforting.

I smile, regarding framed photos above the appliances.

As I stare at the photos, my father inspects another dryer. His hands move like a sculptor considering the geometry of a future statue.

Hands cupped in a 90-degree angle, inspecting the dryer's white edge, he asks Vargas how much he's charging. There are no price tags on these appliances. And knowing my dad, watching him inspect, he's looking forward to bartering. Regarding Vargas' lack of economic labeling, I imagine the feeling is mutual.

"250," Vargas says.

My father releases his hands off the dryer. He doesn't look Vargas in the eye just yet. He considers the dryer in front of him. It's decent, I think, but something about it is off. It's a gut feeling.

My father looks to me.

I look to him.

He nods.

I nod.

He continues to inspect the dryer as I return to the frames and photos that line the walls. I see photos of Michael Jordan posturized in incredible, athletic fashion, portraits of Al Capone, and another one—a well-known photo—that catches my eye.

In vintage sepia, twelve men sit on an outstretched steel beam eating lunch. Beyond and below these construction workers who enjoy a moment of rest, the formative metropolis of New York City is shown. I imagine how breathtaking it must have been for the photographer then, but its grandeur and scope resonates profoundly within me today.

It's a wonderful feeling I get from the photo. Up high, resting on the shoulder of this formative city, the photographer captured the true essence of the structure's foundation.

I focus close on each of the grainy faces in the photo who now must be dead—horizontal. Various expressions of men who didn't regard the photographer, yet focused on each other. Smiling, smoking, and eating, they did not pose for the camera like generations would do today. Instead, they simply existed to prove a point.

"Do you have anything else?" my father asks.

The steel beams that fortified that building in New York City weren't the true foundation.

"Hmm," Vargas thinks.

It was—and always will be—the people that took the time to build it.

Sons.

Daughters.

Mothers.

Fathers.

"Let me show you what I have in the back," Vargas says.

I look to my father and wait for him to see me. Like a phantom tapping his shoulder, he turns to me.

Are you happy?

His eyes hover beyond mine, possibly somewhere else in the past.

He nods.

We'll see.

—

Vargas leads us out of the store and around the building to a nearby garage.

My father and I scan the alleyway on our walk. Once again, I'm thankful for my father's frame. We get to the garage and wait for Vargas to lift the door. As we wait, I look to my father who's processing something.

Grandma?

Vargas?

The peeling paint on the garage door?

I see his heavy brow and try to release some pressure.

"Is everything alright?" I ask him.

My father looks to me and smiles. "Yeah, I just hope we can buy something today."

Today.

A word that hits harder than usual.

Today may be all my grandmother has left.

The hospice nurse who looks over my grandmother explained to my father that it was only a matter of days until the end. The nurse went on to explain that when someone is on the verge of "transitioning" their ears begin to pin closer to their skull, bending back at the lobe. And yesterday, around lunch, feeding my grandmother fresh watermelon, her shrunken ears were the only thing I could focus on.

But now, looking at my father, I focus on him.

"I hope so, too," I say. "And I want you to know that I'm willing to put some money down for you."

"No," he says, shaking his head like a father does.

"Yes," I say, keeping my eyes on him firmly. "Listen. This guy doesn't look like he's going to budge from 250. Let me put in 100. That only leaves you the rest—plus the delivery fee, which, to be honest, will be much cheaper than having him come into look at the old one, asking you to buy an aged part that is probably twice as expensive as one of these machines, and then on top of that charge you a worker's fee. That alone is going to be more than the price of one of these. The least I can do for you, and for grandma, is pitch in. Will you let me do that? Please?"

My father silently regards my words.

A soft breeze dances between us.

"Let's just see what he has, son."

I nod, turning my vision back to the garage.

Another breeze dances down the alleyway where we stand. Transient echoes of life in the form of candy wrappers and plastic cups billow around us like leaves. Eventually, the breeze settles by our feet. And just before the garage opens, my father places a warm hand on my shoulder.

Thank you.

A little startled, I reach up and place one of my own on his.

You're welcome.

The garage door opens.

And the cool breeze remains by our feet

Together, we spot a nice Whirlpool dryer.

My father asks Vargas "how much?"

"250," Vargas says with confidence.

I look to my father and nod.

Are you happy?

My father looks to me—our eyes becoming four structures connected—and I see his response. His eyes elicit some nostalgic quote in me. It's from a film we've watched many times together.

The eyes, chico…they never lie.

And riding back to my grandmother's house, noting tonight's fresh delivery from Vargas, our eyes glance at each other in conversation.

The whole way back they never lie.

—

That night, after Vargas' delivery, the new Whirlpool tumbles softly in my grandmother's basement.

I hear its machinery as I pass the basement door heading for the living room. Although, with two beef sandwiches in hand—one for me and one for my father—I stop at my grandmother's door and check in on her.

Despite the new bed, my grandmother's sound asleep on fresh sheets.

Fresh sheets provided by the new dryer.

"Are you happy?" a familiar, soft voice asks from underneath the sheets.

"Yes, grandma," I say, leaving her to rest. "I am."

My father sits in the living room watching some late-night talk show. I sit next to him and pass him his sandwich. Automatically, eyes still on the television in front of him, he unwraps the beef. I stare at him unwrapping mine. As he eats, I want to ask the question.

Are you happy?

However, he's got a mouthful of beef.

I smile, knowing I'll ask him later on.

Because right now, eating our sandwiches, we're on our lunch break.

Right now, we're a couple of men sitting on a steel beam ourselves.

And tomorrow, we'll have more work to do.

I take my eyes off my father and turn to the late-night show. As I watch Jimmy Fallon throw water in a celebrity's face, my father speaks.

"I love you, son," he says—in-between bites.

"I love you, too."

We continue to watch the show.

And as we watch, I shift my hearing from the television to the background noise of my grandmother's home.

Focusing close, becoming one with the subaudible,

I hear the Whirlpool dryer underneath our feet tumbling away in the basement.

Its sound reminds me of a bustling and growing city.

One—I muse in-between my bites—that isn't sepia anymore.

Acknowledgments

Many people helped *Seasons* see the light of day. To name some of the writers who've inspired me thus far, I want to thank Stephen King, Ray Bradbury, Tobias Wolff, Ernest Hemingway, Noah Hawley, Herman Melville, Julio Cortázar, Jorge Luis Borges, and Scott Snyder. To all of the people who've supported me throughout the creation of this collection: I thank you. I want to specifically thank my wonderful family (*William, Gennelly, Tyler, Matthew, Nancy, Emma, and David*), Hannah Schaffer, Xuan Hu, and all my former students at Wichita North High School who supported my progress as a writer.

And, lastly, I want to thank *you*, dear reader.
Thank *you* for joining me.
Thank *you* for reading.
Thank *you*.

Stay creative.